Finding Home

Denise Janette Bruneau

Finding Home

Denise Janette Bruneau

Finding Home

Denise Janette Bruneau

ZIMBELL HOUSE PUBLISHING
UNION LAKE, MICHIGAN

For permission requests, write to the publisher
"Attention: Permissions Coordinator"
Zimbell House Publishing
PO Box 1172
Union Lake, Michigan 48387
mail to: info@zimbellhousepublishing.com

Published in the United States by Zimbell House Publishing
http://www.ZimbellHousePublishing.com

Hardcover ISBN: 978-1-64390-038-4
Trade Paper ISBN: 978-1-64390-039-1
Large Print ISBN: 978-1-64390-040-7
.mobi ISBN: 978-1-64390-041-4
ePub ISBN: 978-1-64390-042-1
Library of Congress Control Number: 2019902747

First Edition: August 2019
10 9 8 7 6 5 4 3 2 1

ZIMBELL HOUSE PUBLISHING
UNION LAKE

Dedication

Dear Reader,

Thank you for choosing to read this story. While *Finding Home* is a fictional story, it is one of hope, a second chance, and finding love. This book is dedicated to my dear friend, Alex, who has helped to bring wholeness back to my life. I also want to give special recognition to my sweet friend, Barb. She has overcome breast cancer twice and is still an incredible warrior.

I especially want to thank my husband, Mark, for his support for my writing. I also wanted to give a special thank you to Karly Carson, my editor, for her invaluable edits and encouragement. Thank you, Zimbell House Publishing, for all of your hard work and support. I thank God for giving me the desire to write, and through my writing, share a little of His love with my readers.

Blessings to you and your family,

-*Denise*

Chapter One

2012

"He's easy on the eyes," Jen whispered.

Katy's eyes widened as she whispered back, "That's an understatement. The man is gorgeous."

Lacey smiled at her two best friends and nodded in agreement without removing her gaze from the handsome speaker. The lecture hall was filled with the new bunch of third-year medical students starting their surgery rotation at the University of Louisville School of Medicine. The first week, there had been one lecture after another on different general surgery topics along with a few knot-tying and suturing lessons. Until this lecture, Lacey wasn't sure she would like the surgery rotation.

She had heard the stories that were passed down from year-to-year. She had learned which attending doctors were nice, which ones were ruthless, and which ones you never wanted to be stuck with in the operating room.

"Dr. Mudd calls medical students *meconium*," she recalled someone telling her, "That's baby poop." Lacey was both shocked and amused by that.

"Dr. Metzinger always pimps students on rounds. He is merciless. He even makes the guys cry," she remembered a fourth-year student telling her.

Earlier that week, she had been warned, "Don't ever scrub before the attending physician unless you want to be thrown out of the operating room." Clearly, the surgery rotation was a 'survival of the fittest' and a hierarchical, good ol' boys' club. Lacey wasn't sure her assessment was accurate, but it didn't matter to her. She didn't care to fit in. She just wanted to pass the rotation, alive.

Lacey glanced around the room. She saw Jack sitting near the back with his buddies. Her ex looked good, as always. He couldn't look bad with his coal black hair, deep-set brown eyes, and sculpted jawline. Their break up had happened a year before, but it was still hard to look at him.

He looked her way, and their eyes locked for a moment. She half-smiled at him and then looked away, feeling a little sadness. She thought about how she must not be destined for love or a relationship. So far, Cupid's arrows hadn't been working. It wasn't that she hadn't been targeted by Cupid's arrows because she had been, many times. It was just that none of those arrows had stuck.

Two years previously, at the age of twenty-eight, Lacey had come into medical school as an older, non-traditional student. Most of her classmates had entered medical school straight out of college. During Lacey's pre-medical years, at the age of twenty-one, she had married Marco Passeri, who swept her off her feet with his Italian charm. He was wealthy and had given her the impression that he wanted to take care of her, so it made sense to her to drop out of college. Unfortunately, she didn't realize before her marriage to Marco that he was called the 'Italian Stallion' by his friends for a reason. A few years into their marriage, he confessed to several affairs and asked Lacey for a divorce. After the divorce, Lacey had been devastated, but she painstakingly finished college while working full-time. It took several years, but medical school had always been her dream. When she was finally accepted into medical school, she was glad she had not given up.

Lacey and Jack met during the first week of medical school. Initially, Lacey felt an attraction and was excited to go out with him. When she found out he was five years younger than she was, she decided it wasn't a good idea. Jack wouldn't give up, though. He seemed to turn up everywhere she went, whether it was the library, the school coffee shop, or a study group. He also started sitting closer to her in the lecture hall.

One day, Lacey was surprised when Jack came into the lecture hall and sat down beside her. That day, he told her he wouldn't take 'no' for an answer anymore. Lacey gave in. She had to admit that it had been nice to be pursued by a gorgeous, younger man. Since her divorce, she had been praying for God to bring a kind and loyal man into her life. She couldn't be sure, but she had hoped that Jack might be an answer to her prayers. Since he had persisted in dating her, she reasoned that he truly cared for her and would not abandon her like Marco had.

In retrospect, Lacey had to admit that Jack wasn't a bad person. The two of them had split up because they were going their separate ways. Jack was heading to Texas after medical school to pursue a career in cardiothoracic surgery. Lacey had her heart set on staying in Louisville to study Obstetrics and Gynecology. But still, he hadn't asked her to go with him, nor had he tried to stay.

Lacey exhaled, lost in thought, as she looked down at her notes from the previous lecture. Jen and Katy were engaged in a conversation, and she could hear bits and pieces of it. The next lecturer began to speak and was introducing himself. Lacey looked up from her notes, and her eyes widened at the sight of him. The man was so striking that all of the earlier nauseating, boys' club talk blurred into the background. Even thoughts of Jack seemed muffled and distant in her memory.

Dr. George Andreas had black, wavy hair, blue eyes, and olive skin. His build was lean and athletic, and his broad shoulders were captivating. He was magnificent.

Jen and Katy expressed Lacey's own thoughts exactly. "He looks like a Greek statue," Jen whispered to Katy and Lacey. She smiled and fanned herself as if she needed cooling from his radiating heat.

The room temperature had to be sixty-five degrees, Lacey thought, as she shivered and glanced out at the snowy, blustery, February morning. Then she glanced back at Dr. Andreas. She couldn't take her eyes off the man. For a moment, she imagined running her fingers through his silky, coal black hair. Jen was right; the man's presence radiated heat. Lacey could feel her face flushing and her insides warming.

Katy chimed in whispering, "I think I could use a little Greek right now!"

All three girls chuckled quietly. As they did, Dr. Andreas glanced in their direction. Jen and Katy elbowed each other and sat up straight in their chairs. All three women held as still as possible making every effort to keep a straight face. It was obvious that he had caused quite a stir among Lacey's female classmates. There was whispering and giggling all over the lecture hall.

Lacey studied him. Aside from the fact that he was easy to look at, she also loved the sound and quality of his voice. It was commanding and certain. At the same time, it sounded like a sweet melody. She imagined that he probably had a good singing voice. He was talking about plastic surgery and breast reconstruction after breast cancer. As he spoke, his voice was filled with passion and tenderness. Although she was drawn to him because he was attractive, she was more enamored by his compassion for women who had survived that horrible disease. These women had suffered deforming surgeries, and Dr. Andreas was focused on fixing their physical scars while lessening their emotional ones.

Lacey understood the pain behind those scars. Earlier that school year, she had been diagnosed with breast cancer. She was on her family medicine rotation in September when she had undergone a breast biopsy for symptoms most consistent with a benign papilloma. She cringed as she thought back to the day that her surgeon called her with the pathology results. When expecting his call that day, she hadn't been concerned because the odds were supposedly in her favor. She was only thirty and based on her research and her surgeon's opinion, she was sure the biopsy would be benign.

"There is a small focus of cancer," her surgeon said on the phone. At the word, "cancer," Lacey's mind started spinning, and tears erupted. She remembered only a couple other words the surgeon said that day—*lumpectomy and radiation.* The rest was gibberish. All she could think was, *I'm going to die.*

A few days after that conversation, Lacey underwent a lumpectomy, which left her with a much smaller left breast. Then she underwent six weeks of radiation treatments, which burned the skin and deeper tissues. Unfortunately, the skin didn't handle the treatments well. Through a long, painful process, the skin finally healed, but not without extensive scarring. A few months after radiation, she went to see a plastic surgeon for scar revision. Afterward, the scar looked better, but it was still a daily reminder of what she had been through.

Lacey shook off the stressful memories. She reminded herself to focus on the positives. After all, she survived the cancer and was alive. That experience as a patient was going to make her a more empathetic doctor. And now, best of all, she realized she had a reason to talk to this gorgeous man today.

When the lecture ended, Dr. Andreas gathered his things and started walking out of the lecture hall. Lacey waited until he was close to the exit so she could talk to him privately.

She called out, "Excuse me, Dr. Andreas."

He turned and smiled warmly when he saw her. He asked, "Yes, how can I help you?"

He gazed at her as she walked toward him. Lacey noticed slight graying at his temples and guessed him to be about forty. As she approached him, she became nervous and could feel her legs trembling. His blue eyes and intent stare were intimidating, but she found that his countenance was unassuming and inviting.

"Hi, I'm Lacey Bartlett, and I just wanted to tell you how much I enjoyed your lecture," Lacey said, trying to hide her nervous energy.

"Thank you," said Dr. Andreas, giving her a nod.

Lacey asked, "I was wondering, do you ever let medical students watch you operate? I'd be interested to see some of your breast reconstruction procedures." Then she added, "I have personal reasons."

His smile widened as he pulled a pen and paper from his pocket. "I enjoy having students observe my cases. That would be fine. I'm glad you're interested. Here's my surgery scheduler's name and number. Just give her a call, and she will arrange it." His gaze lingered for a moment, as he handed the paper to her. Their hands touched during the exchange, and Lacey felt a surge of warmth go through her.

She politely smiled and thanked him, and then he hurried on his way. Lacey turned back toward the lecture hall. Everyone was gone, and she stood alone for a while in the empty room. Something had happened during her exchange with Dr. Andreas. Something felt different. She wasn't sure what it was, but in that short meeting with the handsome, Greek man, something had stirred inside her soul. She felt connected to him.

A few weeks passed, and Lacey was not able to drum up the courage to call Dr. Andreas' office. The truth of the matter was that she was attracted to him. She didn't want to scrub surgical cases with him. She wanted to have dinner with him, and she was pretty certain that he wasn't married. She had looked for a ring on his finger, but there was none. But she also felt certain that a beautiful man like him probably wouldn't look twice at her. Lacey considered herself pretty, but he was an attending doctor, and she was just a lowly, medical student. Lacey imagined that he was probably dating a refined lawyer who looked like America's next top model. In her mind, she could only envision him with a beautiful and intelligent woman. She could only see him with a woman who matched him in beauty and stature.

As the surgery rotation finished, so did most of Lacey's thoughts of Dr. Andreas. Part of her was glad she had tried to let her attraction for him go, though another part of her still hoped to see him. Many days, she would see him in the hospital halls, just in passing. She was thankful that he would at least acknowledge her with a nod, or a quick wave, but it was never anything more. Each time she would see him coming down the hall toward her, she would hope he would stop and have a short conversation with her, but that never seemed to be on his agenda. Some days, she imagined having a chance to meet with him in a dim, hospital hallway. She imagined that he would accidentally bump into her and almost knock her down, and then catch her in his arms. If only something like that would happen, she was sure he'd look deeply into her eyes and fall in love with her instantly.

Of course, the reality check that followed this fantasy was disheartening. In time, Lacey told herself that this infatuation would fade away.

Chapter Two

In July, Lacey started her fourth year of medical school. On a Friday morning in late August, Lacey sat in the doctor's lounge drinking a cup of coffee. She was between lectures on the High-Risk Obstetrics rotation and decided to get some study time in. She looked around the lounge and noticed the empty tables, chairs, and couches. The lounge was un-characteristically quiet. Usually, there were doctors and students streaming in and out. She looked at her watch to see that it was only nine-thirty. The mid-morning time explained the emptiness of the room, and she knew the traffic of people would be picking up near lunchtime.

Lacey was sitting with her back to the lounge door, and she didn't hear the door open.

"Well, hello, young lady," said a man's voice from behind her.

Lacey recognized the smooth, sweet voice as she turned around. It was him. George Andreas stood smiling at her. He was wearing a dark suit with his white coat draped over his arm.

"Hi," she said, smiling back nervously. As she stared into his eyes, she thought they might be the color of the Aegean Sea. Her breath caught in her throat.

"So, there is a certain medical student who was going to call my office and come scrub some surgeries with me. I'm not sure what happened to her. Do you know her?" He asked raising one eyebrow.

Lacey's expression turned to one of surprise and embarrassment. She wasn't going to tell him the real reason she hadn't called. She couldn't tell him that he intimidated her because she was smitten by him. She felt her face flush as she started to answer, "Oh, yes, that, well ..."

His smile widened, and he shook his head, "I'm kidding with you. I thought you could use a little teasing today. You looked too serious with your nose in that book. I just wanted to see you smile."

Lacey smiled. His jovial manner put her at ease. She said, "I kept meaning to call, but my rotations have been really busy." She didn't make a habit of lying, but she reasoned that her statement was partially true.

He chuckled and then smiled at her. "Don't worry about it. I'm giving you a hard time. I remember what it's like to be a medical student."

Lacey replied, "I just started fourth year. I'll be so glad to graduate."

He started to walk into the kitchen in the lounge and said, "Enjoy this time while you can. Residency is not something to look forward to." He disappeared from Lacey's view in the kitchen for a few moments. When he reappeared, he was carrying a cup of coffee in a white styrofoam cup. "Have a good day. Enjoy this year," he said, as he walked toward the door to leave the lounge.

Lacey smiled back at him, "Thanks for the advice. I will."

As she watched him leave through the door, Lacey exhaled, not realizing she had been holding her breath. She just stared at the door for a few minutes replaying every minute she had just spent with him. Her thoughts were jumbled. On the one hand, he seemed a little flirtatious, but on the other hand, he hadn't said anything about seeing her again. Then she thought, *But the way he smiled at me. There has to be something there. He has to feel something for me.*

Her shoulders fell as she exhaled again, defeated. She realized that she was probably being ridiculous. He was most likely this friendly to everyone, and she was just trying to read something into nothing. A deflated feeling followed. She was obviously smitten with a man who would probably never return her feelings.

She prayed, *Lord, if my feelings mean more than infatuation, and if this man is a good man for me, please bring us together, somehow. But if he is not right for me, please help me to forget about him.*

Lacey looked at her watch and gathered her belongings. Her next lecture was in fifteen minutes, and she wanted to get a good seat in the lecture hall. She picked up her book bag and went to sling it over her left shoulder. As she did, a tearing pain occurred under her left armpit that brought tears to her eyes. She took a deep breath and then moved her book bag to her right arm. The sharp pain resolved, but her left armpit and chest were starting to burn. *I must have stretched some scar tissue,* she thought. Lacey left the doctors' lounge and walked to the lecture hall. Once inside, she spotted Katy and Jen. Lacey walked up the lecture hall stairs to their row and plopped down next to Jen.

"Hey, beautiful lady," said Jen. Lacey loved that Jen always had such a positive outlook on life. She also had a flair for giving people lavish nicknames. Being around Jen usually boosted Lacey's mood and gave her a shot of confidence.

Lacey smiled and asked, "How has your day been?"

Katy chimed in, "Don't get me started. Josh is a horse's rear end." Unlike Jen, Katy had a more realistic way of putting things and was not one to sugar coat anything.

Lacey asked, "What happened?"

Jen shook her head and said, "I'm sure something came up, but last night ..."

Katy interrupted, "That jerk stood her up. Just wait until I get a hold of him."

Jen relented and just nodded.

Lacey said, "I'm so sorry. What is wrong with him? Doesn't he know how to use a phone? Maybe he has a legitimate reason for not showing up."

Katy's face reddened with irritation as she pointed across the room. She said, "A legitimate reason like that brunette over there? I'm seriously going to take him down if he ever tries to talk to Jen again."

Lacey looked where Katy was pointing. Sure enough, Josh was sitting next to some brunette. They were smiling and talking, and Josh was leaning in a little too close to her. Lacey said, "Oh, Jen. I'm sorry. He's such an idiot."

"I know," said Jen. "It's a good thing I didn't really like him. Don't worry, ladies. From my perspective, he's not worth it."

Lacey shook her head back-and-forth and remarked, "I didn't like him anyway. There was always something dishonest about him, and now we know for sure."

The room quieted as the speaker was introduced and the lecture began. Lacey found the topic of risk management to be quite boring, and her thoughts wandered to the Greek man. She couldn't fight her feeling of attraction for him. If only he could see her as a woman and not a medical student. She exhaled as she realized that her wish probably wasn't a realistic one.

She reached for her water bottle in her book bag. As she extended her arm, the tearing pain in her left armpit came back. This time it didn't go away, and Lacey felt like the skin over her left chest wall was on fire. She winced as she leaned forward trying to get comfortable.

Jen leaned over and whispered, "Are you okay?"

Lacey took a deep breath and exhaled. She shook her head, unable to speak because of the pain.

Jen reached for her arm, but Lacey pulled it away as Jen's hand brushed her arm. It hurt, and the pain was now radiating down her arm.

"Lacey?" Jen whispered again.

"My chest and arm," Lacey said.

Jen leaned in and whispered, "Let's go out in the hall to talk. I'll carry your books." Jen leaned over and whispered to Katy, and then all three girls exited the lecture hall.

"What's going on, Lacey?" Katy asked, reaching for her.

Lacey was hunched over, guarding her left arm and left chest. "I don't know. This pain started this morning, but it stopped for a while. Now, it's back, and it's bad. It's constant. I feel like my arm and chest are on fire. It hurts to touch the skin."

Jen said, "It can't be a heart attack. You're only thirty."

Lacey shook her head. "No, I don't think that's it. This is the breast cancer side, where I had surgery and radiation. It may have something to do with that."

Katy said with a forceful tone, "Let's get you down to the ER now."

Lacey didn't argue. Katy took Lacey's right arm, and Jen carried Lacey's book bag as they headed to the ER.

When they arrived in the ER, Lacey was taken back to room fourteen.

As Lacey started to change into a hospital gown, Jen shrieked, "Oh, my gosh! Lacey, your arm!"

Katy looked terrified also and said, "It's so red."

Lacey looked down at her arm. There was a wide streak of redness running down the underside of her arm down to her elbow.

Jen and Katy leaned in to see the redness better.

Katy said, "Raise your arm." Lacey complied but winced with pain.

Jen looked closer and said, "The redness runs up into your armpit." She traced the erythema further to Lacey's chest. "It looks like you may have an infection," she said.

Katy commented, "Your skin feels so warm."

Lacey replied, "But I'm freezing."

Then Katy added, "I bet you have a fever."

As the girls were examining Lacey, the emergency room doctor walked in with a nurse tagging along behind him. "Hi Lacey, my name is Dr. Payne, and this is Amber, my nurse. I understand that you are a medical student?"

"Yes, I was just upstairs sitting in a lecture. These are my best friends, Jen and Katy. They're in my class," Lacey replied.

Dr. Payne nodded to the girls. Then he turned to Lacey and asked, "Can you tell me what's hurting?"

Lacey proceeded to explain her past history of breast cancer, her current symptoms, with onset and duration, and then showed Dr. Payne the redness along her arm, armpit, and chest.

"You have cellulitis," he said. "It's an infection of the skin. Given your recent history of breast cancer surgery, radiation, and scar revision, it makes sense."

Amber leaned toward Lacey to take her temperature. She said to Dr. Payne, "Her temperature is 103."

Lacey's eyes widened. Jen covered her mouth with her hand, and Katy exclaimed, "That's not good."

Dr. Payne said, "This infection is pretty serious. We need to check some labs, start an IV, and get antibiotics started."

Lacey nodded in disbelief. She asked, "Why is this happening?"

Dr. Payne replied, "Radiated skin is tricky. It can become infected easily. I don't see any points of irritation on your skin, though. Have you suffered any trauma to this area?"

Lacey thought for a few minutes. Then she said, "I can't think of any obvious bumps or bruises, but I do carry my book bag on my left shoulder a lot. It actually started hurting this morning when I picked up my book bag and put it on my left shoulder."

Dr. Payne replied, "That might be it." Then he paused, "Who is your plastic surgeon? I need to call him. He will need to admit you to the hospital and treat you with antibiotics."

Lacey replied, "Dr. Esposito did my scar revision."

Dr. Payne nodded and said, "Okay, let me give him a call. Amber will be back to start your IV and draw your labs."

"Thank you," Lacey said.

As Dr. Payne left the room, Amber walked in with intravenous tubing, an intravenous pole, and supplies for a blood draw. She gave Lacey two Tylenol tablets with some water, and Lacey swallowed them down. Amber started the intravenous line, and as she left the room, she said, "I'll be back with your antibiotics."

"Thank you," said Lacey.

Lacey turned to Jen and Katy, "You two need to get back to the lecture. I'm going to be fine. At least we know what's going on. I just need a few days of antibiotics."

"Are you sure you're okay by yourself?" Jen asked.

"I'm fine. I'm in good hands," Lacey replied.

Both girls gave Lacey a gentle hug. Katy said, "Call us when you know what room you'll be in."

"I will. Have fun in lecture. At least I'm getting out of those boring talks today. I'll need to copy your notes later," Lacey replied with a smirk.

Jen and Katy waved one last time as they left.

A few minutes later, there was a knock at the door. Lacey looked up as the door slid open. She was expecting to see Dr. Esposito or Amber, but instead, she saw George. At the sight of him, her heart leapt in her chest and her breath caught in her throat. She tried to speak, but she couldn't seem to form a word.

"Hi, again. We need to stop meeting like this," he said, smiling.

"Hi," Lacey replied with hesitation in her voice. Then she said, "I think you might be in the wrong room."

He looked down at the chart he was holding and asked, "Lacey Bartlett?"

"Yes, that's me," she said.

"I'm in the right place, then," he said.

Lacey furrowed her brow feeling confused.

George said, "Did Dr. Esposito do your scar revision?"

Lacey replied, "Yes, he did."

George said, "Well, he's out of the country for a month, and I'm covering for him."

"Oh," she said.

"Is that okay with you?" He asked when he saw the confused look on her face.

"Yes, of course. I guess I'm just surprised," she said.

He smiled at her and asked, "Is this a good surprise or a bad surprise?"

She smiled nervously at his humor and said, "A good one, of course."

Amber walked into the room and hung the antibiotic bag. She said, "Excuse me, Dr. Andreas, may I go ahead and give her the pain medicine?"

George replied, "I'd rather you wait a few minutes until I examine her. Can you stay while I do the exam?"

Amber replied, "Of course," as she smiled at him and touched his arm briefly.

Lacey saw the exchange between Amber and George. She felt a heaviness in her gut and realized it was a twinge of jealousy. She rolled her eyes at herself for feeling jealous.

"I'm going to take your gown down far enough to expose the cellulitis. I need to see where it starts," George said.

Lacey immediately felt self-conscious. "Um, oh, okay," she said.

"I will only expose what I need to see. Then I'm going to use this ink pen to mark the margins. So I'll be giving you a temporary tattoo," George said smiling, trying to lighten her mood.

"Okay," she replied as she hesitated to lower her gown. To her surprise, he didn't have to expose much of her chest, and she felt relieved. He wasn't in a hurry, and his touch was gentle. She appreciated that since her skin felt like it was on fire.

He gently traced the margins of the redness while explaining to her that the margins should shrink each day because of the antibiotics. After the margins were marked, he replaced her gown and said, "You must have traumatized the skin without knowing it. Dr. Payne told me about your book bag. Radiated skin is very sensitive. If the antibiotics don't help, I may have to open up your scar and see if there is fluid underneath. That fluid may need to be drained if it's the source of the infection."

Lacey's expression became troubled. "You mean, I might have to have another surgery?"

"It's possible, but let's just hope the antibiotics will do the trick."

Lacey nodded.

Amber left the room saying, "I'll be back in a few minutes."

George and Lacey sat in silence for a few moments. Finally, George broke the silence, "Are you okay?"

Lacey nodded.

George said, "You're too young to have to deal with all of this. I'm sorry."

Lacey nodded again and pursed her lips. "I'm okay. It could be worse," she said.

He stared at her for a moment longer as if he wanted to say more, but he didn't. Then he stood and leaned forward to touch her right forearm, "I'm going to go write orders and get your room assignment for admission. I'll be by to see you in the morning. Have a good day."

"Thanks," she replied.

Lacey sat still and stared at the wall for several minutes. She was trying to process the events of the day. She didn't understand how she could have cellulitis months after her surgery scar had healed. She hadn't realized how much damage the radiation had done. She whispered, "Lord, I don't want another surgery. Please let this antibiotic work." She shivered as she started to feel cold again.

Her thoughts turned to George. She couldn't deny her feelings for him. She was enamored. Every moment she was with him made her want more moments with him. She had to be in love, but how could that be possible? She'd heard him lecture once and had spoken with him on three different occasions, two of them being today. How could she feel such strong emotions for a man she hardly knew? She didn't understand the connection she felt to him, but it felt deep, and she knew she was in over her head. Her attraction to him felt like a powerful magnet, and she didn't think she could break loose, even if she tried.

She cautioned herself. She had, suddenly and without choice, become his patient, so this complicated everything. As a medical student, she had been required to sit through ethics lectures about doctor-patient relationships, and she knew they were not wise. A patient could easily misconstrue a doctor's knowledge and expertise as something more than a doctor's care for a patient. She could see how a patient could easily become enamored with a doctor's authority, along with his physical appeal. The patient could then project that the doctor was not only caring for her but that he might have feelings for her, too. She didn't want to fall into this trap.

Then she reasoned that George wasn't technically *her* doctor. He was only temporary coverage. This thought made her feel a little better until she realized that he probably didn't return her feelings anyway. She sighed loudly and then decided she would prefer to dismiss that thought.

Chapter Three

The next morning, Lacey was feeling groggy from the pain medicine. She had experienced sweating alternating with chills throughout the night. Her skin still felt like it was on fire, and she just wasn't feeling well. She sat up to drink a cup of coffee, and there was a knock on the door.

"Good morning," George said, as he stepped inside the room.

"Good morning, Dr. Andreas," Lacey replied, smiling at the sight of him.

As he came closer to the bed, she could smell his aftershave. It was a mix of wood, evergreen, and musk. Lacey inhaled deeply to take his scent in fully. "You smell good," she said, without thinking and felt her face flush.

"Thanks," he said smiling, as he sat down in the chair by her hospital bed. "How are you feeling, Beautiful?" He asked with a big grin on his face.

Lacey could feel her face warming deeper as she smiled and shook her head. "I've felt better."

"Is your pain about the same?" He asked.

Lacey looked at him and pursed her lips. She said, "It actually feels worse."

He nodded and stood up, then said, "Let me look at your skin and my markings from yesterday."

Lacey lay back on the hospital bed.

George moved to her left side and sat on the bed beside her.

Lacey felt her whole body warm as he moved next to her. She was basking in the wonderful aroma of his aftershave when his touch on her arm jolted her back to reality. "Ouch," she cried out and involuntarily pulled away from his touch. "Sorry, that really hurts," she added, looking at him apologetically.

"Sorry," he said, looking at her with gentle eyes. He surveyed her skin a little longer and then made a discovery. "You have a pocket of fluid right here," he said, pointing to an area under her scar.

As he touched the fluid pocket, Lacey winced again and pulled back. "I'm sorry," she repeated. "It just hurts so bad."

"I'm done," he said. "I won't poke on you anymore." He moved back to sit in the chair at the bedside.

"It's worse, isn't it? Why is there fluid? Are you going to have to operate?" Lacey's thoughts came out all at once.

George was quiet for a minute and looked as if he was trying to collect his thoughts. Then he answered, "The infection is spreading beyond the inked margins. This fluid collection under your scar is worrisome. I think the trauma from your book bag caused a small bleed under your scar. It looks like the fluid is infected, and now that infection has spread to your skin, and the infection is worse despite antibiotics."

Lacey felt her anxiety building and asked, "What does that mean? Can't you just change the antibiotic?"

"I wish I could do something that simple." He replied. "Unfortunately, I'm going to need to drain the fluid, send it for culture, and biopsy the tissue."

"Biopsy? Why biopsy? It's just an infection, right?" Lacey asked, looking alarmed.

George pursed his lips and looked down at the floor as if he didn't want to say what he needed to say. Then he looked up at her and said, "I think a biopsy is necessary because I've seen cancer recurrences that present this way. It's probably just an infection, but I think we should be sure."

Lacey felt the color drain from her face. Her cancer had been caught early. She had never imagined it could come back. *It couldn't come back, could it?* She took a deep breath and then looked at George. She said, "Okay, do what you need to do. I don't want any more cancer. I just want to heal and live my life."

He leaned forward and placed his hand on hers gently. "I know this is hard to hear, and I'm sorry. But I promise you that I'll do my very best for you."

Lacey felt comfort from his touch. She wanted to lean into him and have him wrap his arms around her. "What's the plan?" She asked.

He replied with hesitation in his voice, "Well, it's not as straightforward as I would hope. If the biopsy shows cancer, you'll have to undergo a simple mastectomy with removal of some lymph nodes."

"A mastectomy? Lymph nodes?" Lacey exclaimed with pain in her facial expression. "Are you sure?"

George's face mirrored her pain as he said, "Yes, I'm sure. It will be necessary if I find cancer at the time of surgery." He paused, and Lacey didn't say anything. He continued, "I'll consult with Dr. Williams. He is a wonderful breast surgeon. If there is cancer at the time of surgery, he will come into the operating room and perform a left mastectomy and remove some lymph nodes."

Lacey's eyes filled with tears. She looked at him and only nodded.

"Lacey," George said in almost a whisper, "I'll do your reconstruction after you heal. Don't worry, everything will be okay."

That evening Jen and Katy poked their heads through Lacey's half-open door. "Hey, fabulous lady," said Jen.

"We're here to bring you some sunshine," said Katy.

Lacey smiled to see her two best friends. "Hey girls. I'm so glad to see you."

Jen held out a bag to Lacey and said, "We brought you dinner from Stoney River."

Lacey's eyes widened, and she grinned. "You brought me a steak?"

Katy replied, "We know it's your favorite, and we wanted to give you a little TLC."

"You two are the best. Thanks, this is a real treat for me right now," said Lacey.

Jen asked, "So, how are you? What did the doctor say?"

Katy asked, "Do you get to go home soon?"

Lacey's expression changed, and her smile faded. She answered, "No. I'm worse. There's a pocket of fluid under my scar. George, I mean, Dr. Andreas says it's the source of the infection. He's going to take me to surgery in the morning to drain it."

Jen replied playfully, "Wait a minute. I'm not saying your surgery isn't important, but are you talking about gorgeous, Greek statue man?"

Lacey raised her eyebrows and looked at Jen and Katy as they stared back at her waiting for her response. Then she continued the playful banter, "Seriously, you two are more interested in my olive-skinned, dark-haired, Aegean Sea blued-eyed doctor than my surgery?"

Katy and Jen looked at each other then looked at Lacey, "Details, please."

Lacey rolled her eyes and couldn't help but smile. "Dr. Andreas is covering for my plastic surgeon, who is out of the country for a month."

Jen smiled and said, "This is destiny."

Lacey furrowed her brows and asked, "What's destiny?"

Katy replied, "Don't you see, Lacey? What are the odds that your plastic surgeon is out of the country for a month while this is happening? And what are the odds that Dr. Andreas would be covering for him and taking care of you? I mean, you're already calling him George."

"Okay, girls, you're getting carried away. I don't call him George; and as much as you think this is destiny, I'd seriously prefer a date with him in a romantic, Italian pub."

Both girls laughed. Then Jen said, "Sorry, we're just trying to cheer you up. We know this is awful, but we're trying to see a positive side."

Katy raised her eyebrows and added, "And George is definitely a positive side."

Then Jen's expression turned more serious. She said, "Well, if the surgery will help you heal faster, then that's a good thing."

Lacey exhaled, and said, "Well, yes, but Dr. Andreas is going to biopsy the tissue also. He thinks I might have a cancer recurrence. If it is cancer, then I'm going to have a mastec—" her voice trailed off as tears welled up in her eyes.

Jen and Katy moved to each side of Lacey on the bed. Katy picked up a Kleenex box and handed it to Lacey. Lacey blew her nose and wiped her eyes.

Katy said, "Sorry if we were insensitive."

Jen added, "Yeah, you know us. We just wanted to make you laugh."

Lacey replied, "I know. You two are the greatest friends a girl could have. I don't know what I'd do without you, especially since I don't have any family left."

The three girls sat in silence for a few minutes, and Lacey's thoughts drifted to her mother. She had died almost ten years previously from breast cancer. Her father had died in a car accident when she was young, so she never knew him. As an only child, she didn't have any siblings.

Jen broke the silence when she said, "We are your family, Lacey."

Katy added, "That's right. You can always count on us, even if you just have one boob."

All three girls broke out in laughter. When the laughter faded some, Katy winked at Lacey and said, "By the way, when you marry George, you had better ask both of us to be your maids of honor, or we'll fight over the title."

Chapter Four

The next morning, Lacey was rolled back to the operating room in her hospital bed. Her fever continued throughout the night, and the infection was worsening. She felt anxious as she waited for George to come into the room, and she prayed silently. The surgery nurse helped Lacey transfer from the stretcher to the operating room table, and Lacey laid there for a few minutes until the surgery door opened. She looked over to see George walk in.

The surgery nurse said, "Good morning, Dr. Andreas."

George looked around the room and said, "Good morning." He walked over to Lacey and leaned down toward her. Lacey inhaled deeply as she caught a whiff of his aftershave. He had a scrub cap and mask on, but Lacey could see his Aegean Sea blue eyes. His voice was quiet and gentle as he touched her arm and asked, "Are you ready?"

"I guess," Lacey replied, lying still on the operating room table.

George motioned to the anesthesiologist that he was ready. George took Lacey's hand and bent down on one knee beside her so that his face was at the same level as hers. Then he asked her, "So which do you prefer, piña coladas or margaritas?"

She smiled and answered, "Margaritas."

Then he leaned down closer to her face and said quietly, "Me, too."

She stared at his blue eyes. The smell of his familiar aftershave and the touch of his hand were comforting. She could feel herself getting sleepy.

He looked at her and said, "Hey, green eyes."

She smiled, and just before she fell asleep, she said, "Aegean Sea blue."

Later that day, Lacey learned that she had undergone a left mastectomy for a local recurrence of cancer. The good news was that Dr. Williams had removed all of it. Lacey was mostly numb to the fact that she had lost her breast. She wasn't particularly attached to the breast, but it was part of what made her a woman. Having a deformed chest made her feel like less of a woman, but she tried to just focus on healing.

By the fifth day of her hospitalization, Lacey had become tired of being a patient. The pain medication had made her feel confused about what day it was, and she was still in pain. Jen and Katy had been by every day, but all of the days and visits were running together in Lacey's mind. She wanted to go home and to go back to living her life.

On that morning, George came in early to check Lacey's wound. She was only half awake when he sat down beside her to pull back her dressing. Lacey opened her eyes intermittently. She was groggy from sleep and the pain medication. Despite her half-awakened state, she could see how handsome George looked in his suit and tie.

"Good morning," he said.

"Hi," she whispered.

Lacey lay still with her eyes closed while he changed her dressing. She had awakened in a state of depression; unlike anything she had felt before. As George looked at her wound, she was on the verge of tears. Lacey had reached her limit as a patient.

George also wasn't his usual chipper self and seemed to be in a hurry. While he changed her dressing, he reached over her to grab the tape. She felt him lean in close to her, and she caught the scent of his aftershave. He smelled wonderful, and for a moment, this reminder of him was comforting. But within seconds, George was finished with the dressing change and was gone. Lacey reasoned that she had fallen asleep because she couldn't remember him saying a "good-bye" or "see you later." She felt tired and sad. George had been the only highlight of her illness; and that morning, she had missed out on a much-needed interaction with him.

Lacey thought back to her initial diagnosis of cellulitis several days earlier. She hadn't minded spending a day or two in the hospital with antibiotics. George was caring for her, and she enjoyed seeing him and spending time with him. She had believed that the antibiotics would help her.

But now she was five days into her hospital stay. Not only had she overstayed her visit, but she had also undergone surgery, lost a breast to cancer, and the pain medicine was distorting her mood. She wasn't having fun with George anymore, and she didn't feel well.

In her downward-spiraling mental state, she had also come to the conclusion that she had been kidding herself about George. She had no right to see him as anything other than her doctor, and he would never see her as anything more than a patient and a medical student, and a deformed one at that. She began to sob and was unable to stop crying for the rest of the morning. Later that afternoon, she demanded to be discharged home.

Katy drove Lacey home from the hospital and stayed with her for a few hours to visit and to make sure she was okay. After Katy left, Lacey lay listless on her couch. So much had happened in such a short time. She knew she should feel lucky that her book bag had caused trauma to her scar because her cancer recurrence had been found and treated. But more than anything, she just felt lonely. She wanted to have her mom or dad with her to comfort and help her, but they were gone forever. She would give anything to feel her mother's warm embrace or see her mother in the kitchen brewing some hot tea.

When her mother was still alive, and Lacey had experienced a bad day or was feeling under the weather, the two of them would sip on a cup of hot tea together. Lacey longed for even just a smile from either of her parents. Tears erupted and spilled onto the couch. Lacey lay there feeling down and alone. She continued to have episodes of uncontrolled crying the rest of the night before she finally fell asleep from exhaustion.

The next morning, Lacey's phone rang.

"Hello," she answered, still half-asleep.

"Good morning," said George.

Lacey smiled at the sound of his voice and sat up. "Hi," she said, feeling more awake.

George chuckled playfully, and joked, "Are you running away from me? I had to chase you down. I heard you left the hospital."

Lacey couldn't help but smile, and said, "I couldn't stay there one more day."

He replied, "I don't blame you. I know this has to be hard for you. You are one tough lady, though."

She exhaled and replied, "I used to be, but I lost my toughness yesterday."

There was a pause on the line, and then George said, "I'm calling because I need to look at your wound. You still have a drain in."

Lacey started to answer, "Okay. I can make an appointment—" but she was interrupted by him.

"I'll stop by your house after work today and advance your drain. That way you don't have to find a way to get to my office. Plus, I live close to you."

Lacey was surprised that he remembered where she lived since they had only briefly talked about it a few times. She asked, "You mean like an old-fashioned house call? Are you sure?"

He replied, "Yeah, it's no problem. You can't drive anyway. I'll see you tonight."

Lacey replied hesitantly, "Okay. Thank you."

⊱━━❈━━⊰

The doorbell rang around six-thirty. Lacey opened the door to find George still wearing his blue surgery scrubs. He was carrying a black, leather doctor's bag.

"Hi," she smiled and invited him in. "Looks like you've had a long surgery day."

"Oh, just the usual," he said, smiling at her. "How are you feeling?" He asked, standing a few feet across from her.

His close proximity made her nervous. "I think I'm doing a little better than I was earlier," she replied. Then she rolled her eyes and added, "I'm much less dramatic than I was yesterday."

George looked around with some hesitation and asked, "Where is a good place for me to look at your wound? I need good lighting."

Lacey motioned to a kitchen chair, "How's that?"

He replied, "That's fine. Have a seat, and I'll get my supplies out."

Lacey sat down and waited anxiously while George washed his hands and laid out the gauze, tape, and scissors. He put sterile, surgical gloves on and then bent down on one knee beside her. He leaned in close to her as he removed the dressing. Lacey could feel his breath on her neck and felt

- 31 -

flushed. He was kind and gentle, and his presence was comforting to her.

As he worked on her wound, her thoughts of being a defective woman returned. It was probably silly since he was the one who had done the surgery, but she needed him to see her as a woman, not a patient, and especially not a defective one. She wanted to be out to dinner with him instead of having her awful wound be the reason for his closeness to her.

Feeling self-conscious, she turned her head away as soon as he uncovered her wound.

George paused and asked, "Are you okay? Why are you turning away like that?"

Lacey could feel his stare but wouldn't look at him. She felt a lump forming in her throat, and she couldn't speak.

"Lacey?" He asked again.

She didn't want to look at him, because she didn't want to see his eyes looking at her deformity.

"Please, say something," he whispered.

Finally, she choked out, "I'm ugly."

In a gentle voice, he said, "Look at me."

She still couldn't bring her eyes to look at him.

George reached up slowly and touched her cheek. He turned her face to look at his. "Look at me."

Lacey looked at him but couldn't stop the forming tears. She bit her lower lip.

"You are beautiful," he said. A tear ran down her cheek, and George wiped it away gently with his thumb. "I will make this right for you, okay?" He said, and added, "You believe me, right?"

All Lacey could do was nod. She wanted to be engulfed in his arms, but the thought of her defective chest wall made her hold restraint.

George stood beside her and gave her shoulder a gentle squeeze, then he bent down and kissed the top of her head. "You're going to get through this, and I promise you'll be happy when it's all said and done."

Chapter Five

As promised, George worked hard to put her back together. He made a few more visits to Lacey's house until her drain and packing were out. Then over the following weeks, she healed well. Eventually, he performed another surgery on her to place a permanent breast implant. At the end of the process, Lacey was happy with her results and felt like a whole woman again.

During those brief office visits and the hospitalization for surgery, Lacey fell deeper in love with George. She wouldn't admit it when it was happening because she tried to caution her heart. She continued to wonder if he might return her feelings. Although she felt the chemistry between them, she wasn't sure what he felt for her. There were a few times that his gaze held hers for a moment too long, or their hands brushed each other for a moment, or she just caught him staring at her. He had even called her "Beautiful" at one point. There was one time she was sure his face had flushed when she had teased him about something. She didn't know what those things meant, or if they meant anything. She had been afraid to ask since their relationship had been based on doctor-patient interactions.

With her permanent implant in place and no need for future surgery, Lacey no longer needed appointments with him. That meant there would be no more office visits and no more time with him. The thought made her sad, though she realized that this break from a doctor-patient relationship was a necessary one. If there was a romantic relationship in their future, they had to clear this doctor-patient interaction from the air completely and for good.

Lacey did her best to maintain a friendship with George over the next four years while she was in residency. Occasionally, she would pass him in the hallway at the hospital or run into him at a coffee shop. He always seemed happy to see her, but their chats were never long enough for her. To make matters worse, their lives were running in different directions. George had a busy office practice along with a busy surgery schedule. Lacey's life as a resident was busy, sleep-deprived, and stressful.

Lacey found some solace in one benefit of residency training in that it was a good distraction for her. The hours she worked were grueling, and she didn't find much time to dwell on her feelings for George. In her rare downtime, she would try to get together with Jen and Katy, though their respective residency training programs were equally as demanding as her own. Regardless of the distractions, though, she would still find her thoughts drifting to him on rare, quiet moments during the late hours at the hospital. She missed him. She would regularly try to dismiss her thoughts of him and give herself mind-over-matter lectures. They didn't help, though. No matter how much she told herself he was just a professional colleague, her heart wouldn't stop yearning for him.

2017

The years of residency training passed slowly. In May, at the end of her fourth and final year, Lacey was at her condo, sitting in her kitchen on a Saturday morning. Friday had been the last day of her residency, and she had a month off before her graduation ceremony. Graduation day would be such an important event for her for more than one reason. Although it was an accomplishment for her to finish the training, it was also a triumph for Lacey—a triumph over breast cancer and continued survival.

Lacey pursed her lips and looked around the kitchen. She walked to the coffee pot and poured a second cup of coffee. She was still in her pajamas. She loved Saturdays like this one. Days like this had been so rare during her last four years of training. She had only been off a few weekends during that time, and she was soaking up the laziness and comfort of days like today.

She walked into the living room and plopped down onto the couch. Her two-bedroom condo was cozy. She had moved from apartment living when she started her intern year four years earlier. Her condo was quiet and had given her a place of respite from her chaotic, residency life. She was so glad residency was over.

Her thoughts went back to graduation. Although she was excited about it, she didn't want to go to it alone, without a date. She considered asking one of the guys she had previously dated, but the thought just wasn't satisfying. She went through several names in her mind. *No, no, no.* She didn't want to spend that evening with any of them. She truly could not imagine that night with anyone but George.

Though she feared he would say no, she knew she had to at least ask him. After giving herself a long-winded pep talk, she picked up her phone and dialed his cell phone number. Then she hung up quickly, slamming her phone down. "I don't think I can do this," she said out loud. *Lord, give me the courage to call him,* she prayed. She paced her living room floor for a few more minutes thinking about what she would say. "If you don't call him, then his answer is definitely no," she told herself. She picked up her phone again and dialed his number slowly. She held her breath.

"Hello?" George answered on the second ring.

"Dr. Andreas ... George, this is Lacey," she choked out. Her throat was dry, and she felt like her stomach was trying to climb up her throat.

There was a pause at the other end. Then George said, "Hi, Lacey. How are you?"

Lacey exhaled and breathed in again. She cleared her throat and tried to sound more relaxed. She replied, "Oh, I'm fine. Things are good. How have you been?"

"I'm doing well. It's good to hear from you. What can I do for you?" He asked.

Lacey could feel her heart pounding in her chest, and she took a deep breath. He sounded too professional, like a doctor talking with his patient. She pursed her lips and grimaced at the thought of continuing.

"Lacey, are you still there?" George asked.

Lacey exhaled, and with resolve, she replied, "Oh yes, sorry. I called you because I'm graduating from residency in June, and I'd like for you to come with me to my graduation." She could feel her nerves giving way as her face flushed and her skin felt prickly. She knew she was starting to hyperventilate, so she sat down on the couch and started taking slower breaths.

"That's wonderful news. You've been through so much. I'm very proud of you and your accomplishments," he said.

As nice as it was to hear this, the tone of his voice and his statement made her feel as if she was talking to a professor or an attending physician. She had hoped for a less professional response from him, and she had a sinking feeling in her gut.

"When is it?" He asked.

Lacey regained some composure and answered, "It's on June twentieth at seven in the evening at the Seelbach Hotel. It's a black-tie dinner and ceremony." Before making this phone call, she hadn't been sure what she expected him to say. But now, on the phone with him, she was certain he would have an excuse to not be able to go.

George was silent for a few minutes. Then, to Lacey's surprise, he said, "Sure, I can go with you."

Lacey stood from her seat on the couch. Her mouth gaped open, and her eyes widened. She didn't say anything for a few seconds. Then she exhaled, and said calmly, "Really? That would be great." She could feel herself hyperventilating again, so she calmly diverted the conversation to some small talk. After disconnecting the call, Lacey's smile widened. She sat motionless on the couch as she digested this good news. Then she jumped up, squealed with delight, and did a happy dance around her living room.

Jen and Katy helped Lacey find the perfect dress. It was a pale-yellow gown that was sleeveless with an open back. The bodice had lovely beaded detail. It fit her slender figure as if it were made for her. Lacey had her hair professionally done in an updo, and she had a manicure and pedicure done at a local spa. She felt like Cinderella going to the ball. If she had to be honest with herself, though, she was more excited to spend an evening with George than she was to be graduating.

On the night of the graduation, Lacey agreed to meet George at the hotel reception room. He was going to have to come from a previous engagement so he couldn't pick her up. He texted her to tell her that he was running a few minutes late, but this gave Lacey time to socialize with her friends.

As the dinner started, the guests were asked to find their assigned seats. Lacey started to feel anxious and didn't want to sit down without George. Then a thought crossed her mind. *What if he doesn't show up?* She felt a wave of nausea pass through her stomach at the thought of being stood up.

Lacey turned around to look toward the elevator. As she did, the elevator doors opened, and George walked out. Her stomach did a flip-flop at the sight of him. He looked amazing. George appeared to be equally mesmerized with her. They didn't take their eyes off each other, as he walked toward her. He looked like a prince in his black tuxedo. She couldn't believe he was really going to be with her tonight.

His Aegean Sea blue eyes stared into hers as he approached her. He smiled and looked her over. Then he leaned in and kissed her on both cheeks and said, "Wow, Beautiful, you are stunning."

Lacey and George had a wonderful time through the dinner and graduation, and they even stayed up late talking for hours as they sat in the hotel lobby. Their conversation flowed naturally, and they were interested in the same things. They laughed at the same jokes and shared the same sense of humor.

At the end of the night, George walked Lacey to her car in the parking garage and said, "I had a really great time. Thank you for asking me to be your date."

Lacey leaned back on her car, facing George, and crossed her arms. She raised her eyebrow and flashed a flirtatious smile and asked, "Was this a date?"

He returned a knowing smile, and his blue eyes studied her soulfully. "I don't know, what do you think?" He asked.

Lacey's breath caught in her throat. This was the moment she had been waiting for. She had waited a long time to hear him acknowledge that she was a woman he was interested in, not his patient, or just his friend.

He gazed at her, and his facial expression turned serious. He stepped in closer to her. His smile faded, and he leaned in and kissed her lips gently. Lacey's legs felt weak, and her heart started pounding rapidly in her chest. He pulled back and stared into her eyes again. He said, "You look so beautiful tonight."

A long and gentle hug followed, and Lacey whispered, "Thank you for a wonderful night."

George opened her car door, and Lacey sat down in the driver's seat. He leaned in and gave her one more kiss on her cheek. "Good night, Beautiful," he whispered.

Chapter Six

All of Lacey's classmates had accepted jobs with various private practice groups prior to their graduation. Lacey had interviewed with a few local private practice groups and had been offered a job with two of those groups. She wanted to take her time on this, though, since she knew this was a big decision. Although it was nice to have options, neither option felt like the right one. In her heart, Lacey felt like God might be calling her to work in an underprivileged area. She had been praying about it, but so far, she hadn't received any inquiries from rural communities. Whether she was conscious of it or not, she had been putting off the decision to commit to one of the local private practice groups because she thought that God might have other plans for her.

On the Sunday after graduation, a week had passed, and Lacey still hadn't heard from George. He hadn't said he would call, but they had connected during graduation night, and he had kissed her. She was sure he had feelings for her and imagined he was thinking about her the way she was thinking about him. *So, why hasn't he called?*

Lacey couldn't wait anymore. She wanted to talk to George. She dialed his number, and the line began ringing.

"Hello?" George answered.

"Hey, George, it's Lacey. How are you?" She asked.

George seemed surprised to hear from her. He responded, "I'm doing well. I just got back from having dinner with my mom and dad."

"Oh, did you have a good time?" Lacey asked, trying to make small talk.

"Yes, we ate at Martini's. We were all in the mood for Italian food," he answered.

About fifteen seconds of silence passed. Finally, Lacey said, "So, I was wondering if we could talk for a minute?"

"Of course. What do you want to talk about?"

"Did you have a good time with me at graduation?" She asked.

He answered, "Yes, I had a wonderful time."

Lacey said, "I did, too." She paused, feeling the need to know how George was feeling about her. On a desperate whim, she blurted out, "I guess I'm just going to say what's on my mind. I'm wondering why we are so perfect together, and yet we're still not dating each other?" Then, knowing she had started a line of questioning that she couldn't take back, she added, "And the doctor-patient relationship thing is no longer valid. I haven't been your patient for over five years."

George was quiet.

Lacey waited a few seconds, and then she asked, "Are you still there?"

She heard him exhale. Then he said, "Lacey, I know this has been a burning question in both of our minds for some time. I haven't wanted to talk about it, because I haven't been sure what to say."

Lacey felt her heart start to race with hopeful anticipation.

He continued, "I love spending time with you, and I really care about you. The thing is ..." he trailed off as if he didn't want to say what he had to say. Then he continued,

"The thing is, I've been dating someone for the past four years. It's been on-and-off, because we've had some issues, and we just got back together a few days ago. I'm not sure I can give up on her after all of this time."

Lacey was silent upon hearing this news. Her heart sank, pounding in her chest, and she felt like she couldn't breathe.

George went on, "I'm just not sure what to do."

Lacey felt hurt and anger rising in her gut, as she unsuccessfully tried to hold back tears. Although she was disappointed to hear he had a girlfriend, she had never really asked him outright. It made sense, unfortunately, and Lacey knew he was telling the truth.

Finally, after a few moments of silence, she cried, "George, I would like for you to give me—to give us a chance. We are so good together. I really care for you."

George replied, "It's not that easy. Her family has become part of my family. I've taken care of her mother with breast cancer, and they have come to rely on me. It's not easy for me to just walk away."

Lacey felt her heart breaking as tears began to collect in her eyes and roll down her face. His response seemed unfair. *Why would he even mention breast cancer as a factor in his confusion? Can he so easily push aside all that I have been through with my own diagnosis as if it were nothing? What about our connection and the time we've spent together? Does it mean so little to him that he can just walk away?*

"George," she said as she began sniffling, "I like you. I know without a doubt that we would be happy together. I really want you to give us a chance. Do you feel anything for me?"

George was quiet for a few moments. Then he replied, "Of course I have feelings for you. I care for you, and I can't deny that we have a connection. I'm just not sure what to do. I just don't think I can change anything right now."

Lacey asked, "So, you're saying that there's no chance for us?"

He replied, "Honestly, she asked me about marriage yesterday, and we are thinking of getting engaged."

Lacey raised her eyebrows in shock and said, "Engaged? Wow, I didn't see that coming, especially after our date on Friday."

He replied, "I hope you don't think I'm a terrible person. I really do care for you, and this decision has been torturing me. I just don't think I can leave her."

Lacey let out a big sigh, realizing that she wasn't going to change his mind by talking to him longer. Then, with sadness and surrender in her voice, she replied, "Okay, well I appreciate your honesty. Good luck with everything. Goodbye, George." Then she disconnected the call.

Chapter Seven

Over the next week, Lacey went from moments of being okay to episodes of outright sobbing. Her heart was broken. For over five years, she had held onto a glimmer of hope that George cared for her and would eventually see his need for her in his life—as more than a patient or distant friend. But she had been wrong, so painfully wrong. She tried to busy herself around her condo by cleaning and doing laundry. She spent hours on the phone with Jen and Katy. She exercised and forced herself to get out of the house by running errands. She tried to tell herself to be strong and to rise above her heartache. But each day, she fell victim to yet another crying episode.

The second week, her thoughts vacillated between hurt and anger. *How could he have led me on all of these years? Why has he always been so sweet and flirtatious, knowing he had this 'off-and-on' relationship with his girlfriend. Their relationship must have been 'off' for graduation night. How convenient for him.* Then her thoughts would return to the fact that he really hadn't done anything wrong. Then she would break down again.

At the beginning of July, Lacey started receiving phone calls from the two private practice groups in Louisville that wanted her to commit. They wanted her to start work in September, and she needed to complete paperwork for credentialing and insurance to practice medicine with them. Lacey avoided those calls. Her heart was distraught. Both of those practices did their surgeries and deliveries at the same hospital where George worked, and she didn't think she could go to work every day knowing there was a chance she would run into him at the hospital. She couldn't bear to see him, knowing he had rejected a relationship with her to marry someone else. She felt like a big rock had decided to take up residence in her stomach. Its heaviness was almost unbearable, and Lacey felt the need for some kind of relief.

Mid-July on a Saturday morning, Lacey was finishing her morning coffee. She had slept in late, hoping to spend a few more hours asleep and not thinking about George. She wandered out to the mailbox and began sorting through the mail. She was surprised to see a letter from Pocatello, Idaho. *Who could this be from?*

Lacey's mother and father had met in Pocatello and married shortly after that. Lacey was born in Idaho. They had lived with her grandparents for the first two or three years of Lacey's life until Lacey's father was killed in a car accident. She recalled the stories her mother had told her about her father growing up on a potato farm there. Lacey cherished the photographs her mother had given her of her grandparents and her father. Some of the photographs had been taken in their farmhouse and around the farm. Sadly, her grandparents passed away years ago.

Lacey looked at the return address. It was from a law firm in Pocatello; Brown & Brown, P.S.C. She walked inside the condo and sat at the kitchen table. She opened the envelope and started reading the enclosed letter.

Dear Dr. Bartlett,

Please see the enclosed letter from your grandmother, Vivian Bartlett. Please contact me at your earliest convenience.

Sincerely,

Drew Brown, Attorney at Law

Lacey pulled the second letter from the envelope. It appeared to be dated, as the stationery paper it had been written on was slightly yellowed. She surmised it must have been her grandmother's personal stationery because it had hummingbirds depicted in the margins. She remembered her mother telling her about her grandmother's love for hummingbirds. She had shown Lacey a photograph of her grandmother standing next to a row of hummingbird feeders at her farm. There were even a few hummingbirds sipping the delicious nectar from the feeders at the time of the photograph. Lacey's mother told her how her grandmother would visit with the hummingbirds as they ate their lunch in the afternoons. As a young girl, Lacey loved hearing that story over and over, while staring at the photograph.

She carefully opened the letter. The date at the top of the letter told her the letter was over twenty years old. She began reading.

My Dearest Lacey,

If you are reading this letter, I have been long gone to heaven to be with our Heavenly Father. I have thought of you daily since you were born. I remember you only as a wee toddler, though your mother used to send me pictures of you as you were growing up. You are the most beautiful young lady God ever created. When your father passed away, we were so heartbroken, but we were able to find some comfort by spending time with you and your mother. We were so sad when you and your mother moved to Kentucky, but we understood. We knew your mother needed her parents (your grandma and grandpa) to help her through her grief of losing your father. We only wished we could have visited you more.

When your grandpa passed away, I was left to manage our potato farm. I hired a gentleman by the name of Lucas London to manage the farm. I decided to leave the farm to him when I passed away, contingent on the condition that he would leave it to you when he passed.

The fact that you are reading this letter now means that Lucas has passed away. The farm and farmhouse are now yours. The deed is in your name. I have asked Paul Brown, my attorney, to be sure that you would receive this letter and all of the necessary legal documents for the farm.

Don't feel obligated to keep the land or the house. Life goes on, and I'm sure the farmhouse will be worn down and will probably need to be torn down. Feel free to sell the land. It should be worth quite a bit of money. Your mom tells me you have a dream to become a doctor, and I pray that you are able to realize your dream someday. You are a bright young lady, and I know that God has great plans for you.

Your father believed that you were born into this world to make a difference. He used to brag about your spunky personality. He would say, "That girl has some fire in her. She's going to do great things someday." I have prayed that God would use you to share His great love with the hurting people in this world. Please accept the farmhouse and land as a token of my and grandpa's love for you. Your father would be so proud of the wonderful, young woman I'm sure you've become. We are so proud of you, too. Continue to serve God in all that you do.

With all of my love,
Grandma Vivian

Lacey wiped away a tear as it rolled down her face. She couldn't remember her father or her grandparents aside from the photographs, but her heart felt sadness. She couldn't believe her grandmother had left this land and home to her. She could feel her grandmother's love for her through her written words, and it touched her heart.

She picked up her cell phone and dialed the number for Drew Brown.

"Brown & Brown, this is Susan, how may I help you?" Answered a woman's voice.

"Hello, my name is Lacey Bartlett. I received a letter from Drew Brown, and I'm calling him about that letter," replied Lacey.

"Of course, Dr. Bartlett. One moment please," Susan said.

Lacey was placed on hold for a moment, and then she heard a man's voice on the line, "Dr. Bartlett, thank you for calling me."

Lacey responded, "Oh, please call me Lacey. I'm calling you about the letter you sent me from my grandmother."

Drew said, "Yes, I'm glad you received it. What did you think of it?"

Lacey replied, "It made me happy and sad at the same time."

He said, "I can understand. I'm sure it was shocking to you." He paused and then continued, "My father is Paul Brown, and he actually took care of all the paperwork for your grandmother's account. He retired last year and asked me to take over. Mr. Lucas London was caretaker of your grandmother's land until he passed away recently. He was maintaining the property up until a few months ago."

"I'm sorry to hear about Mr. London," said Lacey. "I'm sure he was very important to my grandmother."

"Yes," replied Drew, "She treated him like a son."

Lacey paused, and then said, "What do you need for me to do, Mr. Brown?"

Drew replied, "Please, call me Drew. My dad told me a lot about your family. He was a close friend of your grandparents." He paused, and Lacey could hear him shuffling some papers. Then he continued, "So, Lacey, you have some options. You can come live on your land, sell part of it, or sell all of it. The potato farm has not produced in several years. Mr. London stopped production about fifteen years ago. He maintained the property quite well, though, and I do have a few potential buyers for you." He paused for a moment. Then he asked, "I understand that you are an Obstetrician. Is that right?"

Lacey was still trying to absorb everything Drew was saying. She answered. "Yes, I just graduated from residency."

"Well," Drew said, "I have a good friend who is the CEO of Pocatello Regional Hospital. His name is Griff Moore. He has been looking for a female Obstetrician to join the hospital-employed group here. If you are not tied to Kentucky, you not only have a home here but a potential job offer. The women here would appreciate having you as their doctor."

Lacey felt tongue-tied. Not only did she have property in Idaho, but she also suddenly had a potential job offer in the small town of Pocatello. The thought of moving across the country had never occurred to her. She finally found a few words and said, "Thank you for all of this information, Drew. May I call you back tomorrow?"

"Sure," he said. Then he added, "I hope you don't mind, but I gave Griff your phone number. He'll probably call you soon. The hospital really needs a doctor like you. I imagine Griff will offer you a nice sign-on bonus, and he'll pay for your move. By the way, if you decide to sell off some of your land to one of my buyers, you'll be making a pretty penny."

"How much are you talking about?" Lacey asked as she furrowed her brows.

Drew replied, "Well, you have about five-hundred acres, and then the farmhouse sits on another five acres. My buyer wants to buy the five-hundred acres for a little over one million dollars." He paused and then chuckled, "I guess you won't really have to work very hard in Pocatello if you don't want to, not with that kind of wealth."

Lacey's mouth fell open, and she covered it with her hand. She was in disbelief. She replied, "I'm sorry. Did you say one million dollars?"

"Yes, ma'am. It's one point four million to be exact," said Drew. "The land is at a premium, and you have more than one buyer. In fact, there are a few development companies who've been itching to buy this land for the last few years. The farmhouse is old, but it's in decent shape. It hasn't been lived in for over three months, but like I said, Mr. London was maintaining the place until pretty recently. I'd be glad to meet with you and show you the house, the land, and the offer to purchase."

After Lacey ended the call, she sat still and stared at the wall for several minutes. She couldn't believe what she had just learned. Her thoughts were racing. She had no idea there had been any wealth in her family or that her grandmother had left it to her. She let the implications of this news sink in. With over $200,000 in medical school debt, she could easily use this newly acquired wealth. In addition, practicing medicine in a small town would be a realized dream if she moved to Pocatello. Her current situation in Louisville seemed sad. Her heart was broken, Jen and Katy had recently moved away to take jobs in other states, and she was alone in Kentucky. She really didn't have a reason to be here anymore. "Answered prayer," she said out loud; and at that moment, she knew this was God's plan for her.

She let out a big exhale, then closed her eyes, bowed her head, and prayed, "Lord, it seems that you may be showing me what you want me to do. I hadn't imagined I would ever move from here, no less, move across the country. But if you have a plan for me in Idaho, then I'm willing to go wherever you want me to go. If you want me to move there, please let this job work out, and help me find a home there."

As Lacey ended her prayer, her cell phone rang. "Hello?"

"Hello. Yes, is this Dr. Bartlett?" said a man's voice.

"Yes, this is she," Lacey replied.

"Dr. Bartlett, this is Griff Moore. I'm the CEO of Pocatello Regional Hospital. Drew Brown gave me your number. I hope you don't mind me calling."

Chapter Eight

The next week, Lacey flew out to Pocatello. She planned to meet with Griff for an interview and a tour of the hospital and practice location. She would also go with Drew to the farmhouse and discuss her options with him. As the prop plane descended for landing, the view over the snow-capped mountains was breathtaking. The plane came to a halt at the terminal, and Lacey stepped down the stairs from the plane. The air was warm, and the wind was gusty. Lacey braced her face from the wind as she walked into the terminal. The airport was tiny, but it was quaint and welcoming.

As she approached the baggage area, a tall, thin man approached her with a smile.

"Dr. Bartlett?" He asked.

"Yes," she replied.

The man reached for her hand and said, "I'm Griff Moore."

Lacey shook his hand, and said, "Hi. It's so nice to meet you."

"How was your flight?" He asked.

"It was good. The mountain scenery is so beautiful," Lacey replied.

"Yes, we love our mountains," he said.

"I can't believe how windy it is here," she said.

He replied, "Yes, just wait until winter. The wind can feel brutal at times."

Lacey retrieved her bag, and Griff directed her to his waiting car. The drive to the hospital was only fifteen minutes. Griff commented along the way, "You can get almost anywhere you want to go in Pocatello in less than fifteen minutes."

Once they arrived at the hospital, Griff picked up two coffees in the hospital lobby café. They toured the Labor and Delivery and postpartum floor, as well as the surgery suite and the ER. The hospital was a regional center, so it was larger than Lacey had originally guessed.

Griff explained how the hospital served several surrounding towns, including Chubbuck, Blackfoot, and American Falls. He said it also served the Native American reservation at Fort Hall. Griff briefly described the patient population in the surrounding areas and then told Lacey how much the services of an Obstetrician and Gynecologist were needed. Lacey could sense that he was trying to sell her on the hospital and practice, and she understood why. Although the area was beautiful, there wasn't much to do socially. *This would be a good place to raise a family,* she thought.

At noon, Lacey had agreed to meet with Drew at the front of the hospital. He picked her up in his truck, and they drove out to the farmhouse. Within minutes of the drive, they had left the town behind and were on a lonely, back road. On both sides of the road were acres of brown dirt intertwined with fields of greenery and growing crops. The fields seemed to stretch toward the mountains abutting them at their bases. The mountains reached into the sky and towered over the surrounding valley. There was something comforting about their quiet presence. Lacey couldn't get past the magnificence of the scenery. The clean air and raw beauty were something she knew she could get used to every day.

As Drew turned into a side street off the main road, he said, "The house sits back here." Lacey could see a white, ranch-style house in the distance. To the left of the house was a separate barn-like structure that appeared to serve as a garage, and a carport connected the house to the garage. As they drove closer, she could see that the house had a welcoming demeanor. *It looks so quaint and peaceful,* she thought. Drew drove around a circular gravel driveway at the front of the house and parked the truck.

Lacey got out of the vehicle and glanced around the property. There weren't many trees, and the ones that were there appeared to be more like bushes. She knew this area was considered high mountain desert, but she hadn't expected it to be so sparse of trees. Lacey could tell that the property appeared to be well-kept. Mr. London had done a good job.

Lacey had a mix of emotions as she approached the house. She thought of her mother and father and grandparents. There were probably memories in her subconscious from her younger years that she might never remember. Though, she hoped she would. Perhaps something in the house would trigger memories from her childhood years. Lacey longed to feel like part of a family and hoped that memories of her past would somehow resurface during her time living at the house.

The front door was located on the right side, so the house appeared to run right to left, rather than front to back. The front porch was small and mostly hidden behind several tall bushes. Drew opened the front door, and they stepped into a small room, which appeared to be the foyer. It was more of a square shape. The floor was covered in creek stone, and the walls were covered in thick, wood planks. There was a handmade bench against the wall, and it was situated under a small window. On the other side of this foyer was another door made of wood. It was a heavy, insulated door, and it creaked loudly as Drew opened it.

Drew stepped forward into a large room and then turned to look at Lacey.

He said, "This is the living room, though you can see it's on the large side for a house built during the late 1940s."

Lacey followed him into the room without saying anything. She looked around trying to take it in. There was a familiar smell. She couldn't quite identify its source, but it gave her a feeling of warmth and belonging.

Drew walked toward the back of the room where a French door opened to a screened-in back porch. Lacey followed him and stepped out onto the back porch. She inhaled deeply as the warm breeze rushed through the screens. The air was clean and refreshing. Lacey looked out in the distance at the mountains. She knew they were far away, yet they seemed so close, like visitors who had come to keep her company. Despite their massive size, they gave her a feeling of comfort.

Drew took Lacey for a quick tour of the rest of the house.

He said, "The house is in great shape. As you may recall, I told you that Lucas London maintained the house. He was a builder who specialized in restoring old homes, but since he didn't own this house, he didn't put money into its restoration. He did maintain it well, though, and he even made a few upgrades. I'm not sure if you want to live here, but it would be a good home for you, at least for a while."

Lacey said, "If you don't mind me asking, what happened to Lucas?"

Drew replied, "Well, it's actually a tragic story. He was killed in a construction accident."

Lacy grimaced and said, "That's terrible. I'm so sorry to hear that."

Drew said, "Yes, it was quite sad. I believe he had a son, probably a little younger than you are, and some grandchildren that he left behind."

Lacey didn't say anything. She was lost in thought. She had been here as a child, and it seemed familiar, but she had no memories of it, except for what she remembered from photographs. Despite her inability to remember it, she felt like she had come home.

Drew pursed his lips and looked at Lacey, who was still lost in her thoughts. He said, "Perhaps it's a little outdated for a young city-slicker like yourself. I'm sure you'd like to buy a new house closer to town. I can connect you with a great realtor."

"No," Lacey said abruptly, as her thoughts returned to the present, "I want to live here."

Chapter Nine

Within four weeks, Lacey had flown to Pocatello and sold the acreage of the property. She had also paid off her medical school debt and accepted the job at the Pocatello Regional Hospital. Although the farmhouse was aged, it had good bones, just as Drew had said. Lacey was at peace with her decision to move in, and she planned to have some upgrades done the following spring.

The whirlwind of activity had made her feel dizzy at times, but she continued to push forward, believing that this was the right course for her. Rather than sell her condo in Louisville, she decided to rent it to an incoming surgery resident. She wasn't ready to completely give up her roots in Kentucky. Although she wouldn't admit it to herself, her heart hadn't completely left Louisville.

When she called Jen and Katy to share the news of her big move, they were both stunned initially. The move had seemed so sudden, and they both expressed concern for her living out in a podunk town alone. Jen was now married to a former classmate, Jeffrey, and living in Jacksonville, Florida. Katy met Todd, who was in the navy, after residency. They married soon after and had settled in San Diego. After Lacey explained her dilemma of being alone, her heartbreak over George, and her desire to work in an underserved area, both ladies seemed to agree that this move was the fresh start Lacey needed.

Lacey settled into the farmhouse over the next few months. She left her condo furnished for the surgery resident who rented from her, so she spent some time picking out new furniture for the farmhouse. She decided to go with rustic furniture since it was the best match for the interior of the old farmhouse. Plus, it added a dimension of warmth.

On a cold, November Monday morning, Lacey awakened to the faint aroma of freshly brewing coffee. The aroma intensified as she inhaled deeply and opened her eyes. She looked over at her cell phone. It was six o'clock. She lay her head back on her pillow, feeling too tired to move. The smell of the fresh coffee caught her attention again, and she inhaled.

"Oh, that is divine," she mumbled as she closed her eyes for a minute more. She had set the timer on her coffee pot the night before. Today, hot coffee was the only thing that could lure her out of her warm bed into this cold, Idaho morning. Well, that and the fact that she needed to get to the office. Patients would be waiting for her in the next few hours.

She pondered the events from the last few months, and then sat up slowly and stretched out her arms and legs. She shivered and shrank back under the covers. "Oh my gosh, it's fre-*e-e*-zing!" She yelled.

Two cold months in Idaho and a busy, first call weekend at the hospital were enough to make her want to bury herself under the covers for a long time. Winter was approaching, and Lacey imagined that she'd be sleeping in a snowsuit and boots when it was officially here. She had been warned about the cold in Idaho, but she had apparently underestimated the high mountain desert climate.

Deserts aren't supposed to be cold, right? In this desert, it snowed almost every day between September and May. And, as if the cold temperatures weren't enough, there was dry, frigid air constantly being thrust down into the valley from the Rocky Mountains. The wind gusts were intense at times and had blown a plethora of tumbleweeds up against her back porch. Lacey found this phenomenon to be both annoying and a bit of a strange sight. *Cold in Idaho, yes, but tumbleweeds? Aren't tumbleweeds supposed to be found in hot, arid environments like Texas?*

She grimaced as she peeked out from under the covers and felt the cold of the room on her exposed face again. For a moment, she stared at the vaulted ceiling and pondered how she would get rid of those problematic tumbleweeds. Then her mind wandered to her office schedule. She had only been working at the Pocatello office for one month, and already, her schedule had been double-booked most days. She now understood why the hospital had insisted that she start working as soon as possible.

Her thoughts drifted away as she glanced over to look out the window. It was still dark outside. The room felt peaceful. But in the quiet, she felt lonely. Lacey turned on her bedside lamp. She glanced at her dresser and caught a glimpse of a framed photograph of her and George from her graduation. Her thoughts drifted to George. She felt the familiar ache in her heart. She missed him, and it didn't help that she still kept a picture of him on her dresser. *Please help me move past George, Lord.* Frowning, she exhaled and decided that the least stressful topic to dwell on this morning was the tumbleweeds.

She yawned with sleepy eyes as she mumbled, "Need coffee." She slipped on her slippers and robe and stood from the bed. As she walked by her dresser, she picked up the framed photograph of her and George and turned it face down. She stepped out into the hallway and made her way to the kitchen. The farmhouse was a large house compared to a standard home built in the late 1940s, though it wasn't much bigger than Lacey's condo back in Kentucky. The kitchen was small, with outdated appliances along one wall, and a narrow bar area on the other side. There was an opening in the wall above the bar area that opened into a formal dining room. Just inside the kitchen from the hallway was a small table that sat snugly under a large, kitchen window. The kitchen floor was covered with wide wood planks.

Lacey pulled a coffee mug from the cabinet. The house was quiet as she glanced out the kitchen window. She could see the outline of the base of the mountains, though it was still dark out. During daylight, the majestic Bannock Range of the Rocky Mountains could be seen in the distance. The mountains were made mostly of limestone, but their coverage was full of green vegetation, forests, and streams. The Bannock Range had been named after the Bannock Indians, who had first climbed the range and lived at the foot of the mountains. Many of their Native American ancestors still lived locally at the Fort Hall Indian Reservation located between Pocatello and the close town of Blackfoot.

Lacey's grandparents had appreciated the beauty of the mountains. She assumed this was why they had built the elegant porch that spanned a large portion of the back of the house. When she first moved in during the summer months and the weather was warmer, she had spent every morning sipping her coffee on the porch.

During the summer, the mountains feigned hues of green, red, brown and gray, and the clouds encircled and hovered over the highest peaks. Their beauty was beyond words. For Lacey, they had represented a quiet comfort and peace she knew she needed, as if they were a gift from God. When she had seen this raw beauty from the porch, she knew this was going to be home for her.

She glanced out at the mountains again with sleepy eyes and a quiet sigh. It was still fairly dark, but she could see that it was snowing again. She poured a cup of coffee and added sugar and cream in just the right proportion. She closed her eyes with the first sip as she tasted and almost breathed in the flavor.

"Mmm," she exhaled as she felt the warmth of the coffee in her stomach.

She walked down the hallway to the living room. The living room was wide with vaulted ceilings, and the floors were covered in wide, wood planks. The flooring added a hint of ruggedness, and there were several thick, wool rugs sprinkled throughout the room. The rugs added just the right amount of warmth to the room and a little for her feet.

Toward the front of the room was a big, picture window. On the adjacent wall was a large, brick fireplace. It had once been a wood burning fireplace, but it had been converted to gas at some point. Lacey was glad for this, as she reached over and turned on the switch for the gas fireplace. She sat on the hearth for a few minutes warming her back.

She stood up and took a seat on the soft, brown leather couch she had bought for the room and sank down into the corner leaning against a pillow. The leather was cold, so she threw a blanket over her legs, reminding herself that leather probably wasn't the wisest choice in this climate.

The couch faced the picture window at the front of the room. Lacey stared out the window at the grand, mountainous view and continued to sip her coffee while warming her hands on her mug. Little rays of light could be seen peeking through the clouds, as the sun was starting its ascent into the morning sky. The clouds were still low, but thin, as they encircled the mountain tops. Outside, the snow continued to fall peacefully and looked like soft, white powder floating to the ground.

While seated on the couch, Lacey peered into her small office just off the living room. French doors opened into the space, and faint rays of sunlight from the front windows glistened onto the wood floor. She had been using this space to read for work, pull up patient charts, and review fetal heart tracings. She had hung her college, medical school, and residency diplomas on the walls behind her desk. Drew had told her that the room had been used as a men's grill, back before her grandfather's day. The whole room was covered in wide wood planks and stained with a dark mahogany color.

Lacey's desk was a simple writing desk made of medium cherry wood. It had slender, curved legs and only one drawer centered in the middle. There was just enough room for her laptop and a few other desk toppers, including a nameplate made from stone that read, "Lacey Elise Bartlett, M.D."

Next to her desk, she had placed a dark mahogany bookshelf, on which all of her medical books lined the shelves neatly. She stared at her diplomas. It was hard to believe that she had spent twelve years in school to become a doctor. Her last hurdle had been to pass her board certification exam for Obstetrics and Gynecology, which she had done recently, in September.

She stood and walked past the French doors back toward the kitchen for more coffee. As she walked down the hallway, there were two bedrooms and a bathroom to the left, while the master bedroom was off to the right. There was an additional hallway off to the right that led back to a separate room with a fireplace. Drew told Lacey that this room had once been a tea room or sitting room for ladies. The floor was covered in polished, narrow wood planks, and the walls were covered in a beige-colored plaster. A beautiful, crystal chandelier hung from the ceiling, and several windows overlooked the porch and what appeared to be a garden, at one time.

Lacey had decided to purchase a pool table and put it in this room. It was a beautiful piece of furniture for the space. The cherry wood of the pool table with its taupe felt was a nice contrast to the dark wood flooring.

Lacey was not a pool shark, by any means, but she always wanted a pool table. During her residency training, she and her friends would play pool as a way to unwind and relax together. She enjoyed the slow pace and mindless concentration of shooting the balls into the pockets. In Louisville, she had not been able to afford a pool table, nor could her condo accommodate one. This room, with its space and gas fireplace, seemed to be the perfect place for one. She had already come home several days after office hours to shoot pool and sip on a glass of wine by the fire.

Lacey walked into the kitchen and smiled as she thought about the last few months. She poured another cup of coffee and then meandered back to the living room to sit near the fireplace. Although she still missed George, she felt like she had come a long way emotionally. When she had learned about his girlfriend during the summer, her heart had been thrashed, and she had felt like a broken person. Now, several months later, she was relieved to have an answered prayer. She had a new start in a new home across the country. This new start had been the nourishing and healing medicine her broken heart needed, and she believed she was healing.

When Lacey had first learned about the farmhouse, she considered selling it; but after her initial visit, she felt drawn to it. For her, it represented the only family she had. Even though it needed central heating and air, new appliances, and a lot of work, Lacey knew this was where she belonged.

She knew that she was getting a fresh start, no matter how worn or withered the farmhouse appeared. It was home.

Despite the peace she felt in her home, she still craved companionship. She loved the seclusion of the house, but it left her feeling lonely at times. She wanted to share her life with someone. She wanted a family. She wanted to have kids running around the house making noise. *Please, Lord. Someday.*

She thought of George, again. Although she had been so in love with him, it hadn't mattered. He did not love her back. She could remember thinking that if she was just prettier, or had blonde hair instead of brown, or was skinnier, or just looked more like his girlfriend, then maybe he would have paid more attention to her. But truthfully, she didn't want to have to try so hard to be loved by a man. She just wanted to be loved for who she was. It shouldn't be hard to be loved by someone.

Praying for a husband had been near the top of her prayer list for several years. In her mind, George was supposed to be that man, but it was clear that he was marrying someone else. She would just keep praying and believing that God had a plan for her, one that included a husband. She grimaced as she thought about this. At thirty-six, she couldn't help but feel like her biological clock was ticking. On top of her aging self, she wasn't sure she could give her heart away again.

Lacey exhaled and stared down at her empty coffee mug. Although she had been surrounded by a flurry of activity over the past several months, she still felt empty. She stood and took her mug to the kitchen sink, and then she headed to her bedroom to get ready for work.

Chapter Ten

Despite the appearance that Lacey lived in the boondocks, her drive to the hospital was only about fifteen minutes. The scenery on the way was picturesque, with mountain views in every direction. Lacey felt surrounded by the mountains as she drove. At the hospital, the beauty continued. She could look out any window there, and the distant mountains would be in view like beautifully rendered paintings hanging on the walls.

Before going to her office, Lacey took the elevator up to the postpartum care unit to check on her hospital patients. After she finished hospital rounds, she stepped into the elevator to head to the lobby. As she stepped out of the elevator to round the corner, she was stopped abruptly by a man speeding past her. He seemed to be in a big hurry as he whipped by her, bumping her arm and knocking her purse off her shoulder onto the floor. She noticed a blue flash as he zipped by her, and she saw he was wearing blue scrubs.

"Hey!" She yelled as she caught a glimpse of his face.

He yelled back without stopping, "So sorry," while running backward, sideways, and then off at full speed.

"Well, that was rude," Lacey muttered as she picked up her purse and rubbed her arm. She let out a big sigh and then continued on to the coffee shop just inside the hospital lobby.

Maria was working in her usual spot behind the counter. "Good morning, Dr. Bartlett. What can I get for you today? The usual mocha?"

Lacey smiled at her. It was good to see a friendly face after almost being mowed down by Mr. Rude. "That sounds great," Lacey replied, still rubbing her arm.

Maria was a very cute, petite lady in her early twenties. She had short, curly brown hair with long bangs that hung over her eyes intermittently. Every few minutes, she would blow them off her face while tilting her head back. Given the fact that she was a nursing student, she usually had enthusiastic and sometimes unusual questions for Lacey.

Maria handed Lacey her mocha and said, "Have a nice day, Dr. Bartlett."

Lacey replied, "Thanks, Maria. You too."

Lacey took her mocha and crossed the pedway from the hospital lobby to her office building. The pedway walls were mostly windows, and the mountains could be seen on both sides. As Lacey walked toward her office, she inhaled the scenery once again. She didn't think she'd ever be able to get enough of it. She felt content and smiled until her thoughts landed on George. Then instant sadness swept through her heart. *Why am I still thinking about him?*

"Good morning, Dr. Bartlett," said a voice from behind the reception desk at Lacey's office.

Lacey looked over and smiled, "Good morning, Barbie." Barbie was a sweet, really pretty, trim lady in her early fifties. She had short, sandy blonde hair and big, blue eyes. She had decided later in life to get braces. As she smiled, and although they were clear, you could see them glistening on her teeth. She had worked at the clinic for twenty years.

Barbie had helped Lacey with so many details and issues in her first month at the clinic. She had also become her best friend in Pocatello. Barbie knew almost everyone in town, and although she was not a gossiper, which Lacey loved about her, she could tell Lacey almost everything about anyone if she asked. Barbie seemed to almost bounce with energy. She had been a breast cancer survivor for fifteen years, and her positive, upbeat view on life was evident every day. She had a kind demeanor and a humble heart, and her laugh was contagious.

Lacey had already been invited over to Barbie's house a few times for dinner with Barbie and her husband, Darrell. They were like one of those cute couples that actors might portray on a sitcom. Barbie was full of stories, questions, and comments and was just a great conversationalist. Darrell, on the other hand, had a very quiet but sweet demeanor. He really didn't say much, but he would chide in occasionally with his side of a story, or he would add to Barbie's stories. They loved to cook new meals together using different recipes, and they enjoyed trying new wines. Having dinner at their house always meant a delicious, melt-in-your-mouth meal with a matching wine perfect for the palate. For sure, anyone could see that they really loved each other. There was an unspoken sweetness between them, and Lacey hoped for a relationship like theirs someday.

"How are ya today? Staying warm with some coffee, I see?" asked Barbie cheerfully.

Lacey smiled and then sighed as she replied, "I was doing pretty good until Mr. Rude about dislocated my shoulder this morning."

Barbie raised her eyebrows and said, "What? What happened?"

Lacey relayed the details of her hallway encounter with Mr. Rude to Barbie. Barbie tried to figure out who the guy might have been based on Lacey's description, but Lacey hadn't gotten a good look at him.

Lacey smiled at her again and said, "I'm okay. More than anything, my pride was wounded. How are you this morning?"

Barbie smiled, and her braces shined on her teeth. "Oh, I'm good. Your first three patients are here, and Mrs. Jarmin thinks she's having contractions," she said as she handed Lacey the first chart. Then she added, "I was here for her first two pregnancies. She has really fast labors. You'd better go see her now."

Lacey took the chart from Barbie and opened it to review it. "Okay, thanks. I'll see her first then," said Lacey smiling back at Barbie.

Lacey dropped off her purse in her office and then wandered down to exam room two.

Lacey had been told that the patient population in Pocatello and its surrounding areas was unique. It was true that if groups of people intermarried consistently, over a period of time, the gene pool would become more limited. This could easily explain the lofty number of high-risk pregnancies Lacey had already encountered. So far, she had seen pregnancies complicated by blood pressure issues, history of fetal loss, history of deep vein thromboses, and diabetes. She knew she had her work cut out for her. Not only was she going to be busy because of the acuity of the pregnancy problems here, but she was also the only female doctor in this group of six doctors. This news had obviously been marketed long before she had arrived, and her schedule had been packed from day one of her office hours.

Lacey saw patients all morning and was starving by one o'clock.

"Have you eaten lunch, Barbie?" Lacey asked as she walked up to the reception desk.

Barbie looked up from the reception desk. "Yeah, I usually bring my lunch. Darrell makes it for me," she replied.

That's so sweet, Lacey thought. "How is the cafeteria food here?" She asked.

Barbie grimaced, "Well, I guess it's not that bad for a hospital."

Lacey smiled, "I'm so hungry, I think I could eat a cow right now."

Barbie laughed. "Go eat. Your next patient isn't until two-thirty. You need to eat," she said with her 'mom voice.'

Lacey winked at Barbie and then headed to the cafeteria.

In the cafeteria, Lacey stood for a moment, surveying the menu on the wall. Finally, she stepped up to the counter and ordered a turkey burger with French fries and a water.

The lady taking her order asked, "Do you want fry sauce with that?"

Lacey just stared at her for a moment. "I'm sorry, what?" She asked for clarification.

The lady said, "Fry sauce."

When Lacey continued to stare at her with a confused look on her face, the lady studied her, "You're not from around here, are you?"

Lacey shook her head, "No, I just moved here a couple of months ago."

Before the lady could say anything else, Lacey heard a man's voice from behind her, "Fry sauce is ketchup and mayo mixed together. People here dip their fries in it instead of ketchup, but I wouldn't recommend it."

Lacey turned to see who it was. As she tried to focus on his face, she wasn't sure, but she thought she might have seen him before. *That voice*, she thought. Then it dawned on her. It sounded like Mr. Rude.

Before she could get a good look at him or say anything else, he stepped forward past Lacey and said, "Excuse me one second."

Lacey felt forced to step aside.

Mr. Rude asked the lady, "Mikki, you got my order?"

Mikki immediately smiled at him and handed him a bag, winked at him, and said, "Yep, doll, it's the usual. You must be swamped today."

Then he said, "It's a crazy, busy day. Thanks."

Mikki winked at him, and then he was gone before Lacey could say a word. Lacey couldn't believe it. Twice in one day, Mr. Rude had lived up to his name. He had almost knocked her to the floor in his major haste that morning, and now he was cutting in line and talking to her as if nothing had happened earlier.

She shook her head not understanding how people could be so obtuse sometimes.

At the end of the afternoon, Lacey was finishing up her paperwork when Barbie popped her head through Lacey's slightly opened office door.

"How are ya holdin' up?" Barbie inquired with an empathetic smile. Although Barbie was homegrown in Pocatello, she had somehow managed to sound like she was from the Southeast.

"I'm tired but still going. How about you? You're just as busy as I am on this team," Lacey chided back with a smile.

"Yeah, I'm pooped. Hey, Darrell and I are trying a new recipe tonight for dinner. Want to come over?" Barbie asked.

"Oh, that sounds so good, but I'm going to head back to the farmhouse. I think I have a hot bath in my future. I'll definitely want a raincheck if that's okay?" Lacey answered.

"Of course. Sounds good. So how is everything goin' with the farmhouse?" asked Barbie.

Lacey replied, "You know, I realize I just moved across the country, and I have totally new surroundings, but this house feels like home."

Barbie smiled and said, "I'm so glad ya feel that way. We love havin' ya here. I love havin' ya here. Now, we just need to fix ya up with a nice young man. We need to make sure ya stay here."

Lacey shook her head and said, "No, please don't fix me up with anyone. There are already too many moving parts in my life. I need to get settled." Lacey paused, and then she said, "I'm still getting over a heartache anyway."

Barbie looked at her with empathy, "Ya look so sad, Dr. B. Ya know, the best way to get over a heartache is to jump into a new relationship."

Lacey looked at her with alarm in her face, "Oh, no, Barbie, please just let me take my time."

Barbie laughed, "I'm kiddin' with ya. I wouldn't push ya to do anything ya didn't wanna do. Remember, I said we're tryin' to keep ya here, not push ya away."

"Thanks," Lacey replied looking relieved. Then she wrapped her arms around herself and added, "I'm heading home to soak in a hot bath. I can't seem to get warm in this climate, and a hot bath is the only thing I can do to keep from shivering all the time."

Barbie smiled and nodded as if understanding. "Yeah, I still do that sometimes too, and I've lived here my whole life." Then she added, "Well, I'll get going so you can finish up and get home. See ya in the morning, Dr. B. Have a nice evening."

Chapter Eleven

On Friday morning, Lacey woke up at five thirty, had her coffee, and did her morning ritual quickly. She had an early morning meeting with the surgery manager. She would be adding gynecologic surgical cases on the schedule and needed to talk to the surgery manager about what instruments and preferences she had.

She looked outside. It was snowing, again, and she could hear the wind gusts hitting the side of the house. *There are easily five inches of snow on the ground,* she thought. She was glad she could park her SUV under the carport, so she didn't have to remove the snow from it every morning.

Her 4-wheel drive SUV easily maneuvered the roads on the way to the hospital. She pulled into the parking garage and parked in a "Physician" spot. In the hospital, she stopped by the coffee shop to say hello to Maria, but Maria was off for the weekend. Lacey ordered a small mocha from an older gentleman behind the counter and then headed to her meeting.

As she arrived at the surgery manager's office, she stopped by a desk where a man was sitting. He was looking down doing some work and must not have heard her approach because he didn't look up when she walked up to the desk.

"Excuse me," Lacey said.

The man looked up at her and smiled, "Hi, can I help you?"

His voice sounded familiar to Lacey, as her eyes locked with his big, brown ones. She immediately noticed how striking he was. Then her breath caught in her throat, as she realized who he was. *Mr. Rude.*

Mr. Rude was gorgeous. Almost as if she had been nudged, she took a step back as her stomach fluttered, and she felt dizzy. She felt her cheeks start to flush and she started to speak, but it sounded more like stammering. Embarrassed and as red as scarlet, she pretended to look in her purse for something while she tried to regain her composure.

"Uh, yes … I … I'm Dr. Bartlett. I have a meeting with Geret Blake." She took a deep breath and looked back up at him.

"You found him," he said with a big grin, as he stood reaching to shake her hand. "I've been expecting you."

She stared at him for a moment. His dark brown hair made his brown eyes appear almost black. His face had perfect symmetry with a sculpted jawline. When he smiled, Lacey could see dimples on both cheeks. As he spoke, his lips were full, and she couldn't help but look at them.

Oh my, Lacey thought. She took a deep breath as she shook his hand and forced a smiled.

Before she could say anything, Geret said, "I think I owe you a few apologies. I'm pretty sure I almost knocked you over the other day in the hospital."

Lacey had halfway recovered by now, and she said, "Yes, that was yesterday."

"Right," Geret replied adding, "I'm truly sorry. I was running to help with a trauma." Then he added, "And in the cafeteria the other day."

Lacey interrupted again, "Yesterday also."

Geret smiled, "Yes, yesterday, sorry. Mikki usually has my order just sitting on the counter waiting for me, but I guess she forgot. Usually, I'm not in that big of a hurry, but there was ..."

He trailed off, as Lacey finished his sentence. "Let me guess? An emergency?"

Geret smiled with a cute, boyish grin, still with her hand in his grasp, "Yes, I'm very sorry."

Lacey studied him more. He was tall, about six feet, and he seemed to tower over her as he stood opposite her. His hand was large, warm, and strong, yet his grasp on her hand was gentle.

Geret released her hand.

Lacey said, "Oh, not a big deal. Forget about it. If anyone understands emergencies, I do." Lacey felt out of sorts and the need to gather her thoughts. *Classic tall, dark, and handsome*, she thought to herself, as her gaze was glued to his face.

She took a sip of her coffee to calm her insides. *No*, her line of thinking continued, *That description doesn't quite fit him.* Her knees felt a little wobbly, as she stood at the desk with him. At one point she rested her chin on her hand with her elbow propped up on the desk, as if that were going to help her keep her balance.

Lacey considered herself as more of a refined lady, and *hot* wasn't a descriptive adjective she normally used. But she couldn't come up with another exact descriptor at that moment. She just stared at him without speaking.

"Is everything okay?" He asked, furrowing his brows.

"Yes, fine," she said quickly. "Debonair," she said out loud accidentally. Her eyes grew wide.

"Sorry?" He asked.

Lacey shook her head and said, "Nothing, uh ... my friend Deb told me I'd find you here." She exhaled as she tried to regain her composure.

"I don't think I know her," he said.

"Oh, it doesn't matter. I found you," she said smiling, trying to shake off the comment.

"You sure did," he said, trying to match her playfulness.

Lacey pulled her shoulders back and stood up straighter. She cleared her throat, trying to be more professional, and asked, "So I understand I need to talk to you about my surgery requirements?"

He motioned to a chair and said, "Yes, thanks for coming by. Have a seat over here, and we can talk. Let me just get out my list."

Lacey walked past Geret to sit in the chair he had pointed out.

She felt his hand brush the small of her back, as he guided her to a different chair, "Sorry, I meant this seat. That one is on its last leg."

A million prickles ran up her spine as he touched her. Her legs suddenly felt weaker, and she was glad to sit down, because she was certain her legs were about to give out.

"So, how do you like Pocatello?" he asked, as he sat in a chair directly across from her with a pen and paper in hand.

"Oh, it's definitely colder than I imagined, but I'm getting used to it," she blurted out.

Geret glanced for a split second at Lacey's exposed knees. "You're going to turn into a popsicle here if you keep dressing like that," he said, smiling. He added, "The cold will sneak up on you if you're not careful."

She suddenly felt a little self-conscious when she realized her legs were in Geret's view. She had worn a knee length skirt with long boots, and when she sat down, her bare knees were in sight. Lacey crossed her legs awkwardly trying to hide at least one knee. "Yes, it definitely takes some getting used to," she replied, feeling that her face was flushed again.

"You just have to dress for the weather and try to enjoy the beauty," Geret replied, still smiling and seeming to be at ease.

Lacey commented, trying to divert the attention away from her exposed knees, "I am in awe of the mountains. I can't believe how beautiful they are and that I get to see them every day."

"They are magnificent, aren't they? I never get tired of them," Geret replied. Then he asked, "So you're here from Kentucky, right?"

Lacey replied, "Yes. Louisville, Kentucky."

Geret asked, "Have you ever been to the Kentucky Derby?"

Lacey smiled and replied, "Absolutely. If you live in Kentucky, especially Louisville, the Derby is a must-see. The horses are stunning and fast, and the crowds are all decked out in lovely attire. The women's hats are my favorite part."

Geret smiled as he saw her face light up as she talked about her hometown. Then he studied her inquisitively and asked, "So, what brought you out here?"

Geret didn't have a northern accent, but Lacey really couldn't place his accent, or lack of one. She thought for a moment and then answered, hesitantly, "Well, I … I needed a change of scenery. I inherited a farmhouse and some land in Pocatello from my grandmother. Then I found out that the hospital was recruiting for a doctor, and so, here I am."

He studied her for a few seconds more, as if he was trying to see her thoughts, "You needed a change of scenery, huh?" He asked with an inquiring look and added, "Seems like a long way to travel just for that. Did you bring a family with you?"

She couldn't help it as her expression changed to sadness. She shook her head back-and-forth and said, "No, it's just me. I don't have any family."

Geret raised an eyebrow and asked, "You don't have any family?"

Lacey smiled at him and tried to respond playfully, "Nope, it's just me. But the farmhouse was in my family for years, and now it's mine. So, it's kind of like I've come home."

He smiled at her empathetically and, "Well, welcome home then."

Lacey nodded and said, "Thanks."

Geret smiled at her again. Then, he stared off into the distance, as if he were lost in thought. At last, he said, "Sometimes it's best to leave bad memories in the past. It's nice when you can put distance there, too."

Lacey looked at him. His affect had changed. He seemed sad. She started to ask him about his family when he interrupted her.

"Well, let's get this list of your surgical preferences taken care of." He looked down and started to write some notes on the notepad he was holding.

While Geret wrote, Lacey's eyes explored his broad shoulders and arms. He was wearing a short-sleeved, blue scrub top. His deltoids were massive, and his biceps and triceps were bulging out of the short sleeves to the point that he had rolled the short sleeves up. *For sure, he has to lift weights.* In fact, he looked like he might have been a football player at one point, or maybe he still was.

"Is everything okay?" he asked, looking at her.

Lacey realized she had been gawking at him. "Oh yes, I was just wondering if you played football in college? You're … a very big guy," she asked clumsily, trying to recover from her moment of awe.

He gave her a boyish, almost embarrassed half-smile, and replied, "Yep. I played at Idaho State University. I was a middle linebacker."

Lacey tried to be as business-like as possible, as they finished discussing her instrument needs and preferences. As she turned to leave, Geret smiled at her. She noticed that his dimpled smile lit up his whole face. He was a large, intimidating size, but he seemed gentle and authentic.

"Nice to meet you, and I'll see you around. I'm looking forward to working with you," he said as he shook her hand again. Then he added with a sincere tone, "Good luck with your new adventure. I hope it's everything you hoped it would be."

Geret's dark eyes met and held her gaze. She was unsure, but for a moment, she thought she saw that hint of sadness in his eyes again. She glanced down at his hand still wrapped in hers. Again, she couldn't help but notice its strength and size, yet she only felt its gentleness and warmth. Their hands stayed interlocked for a moment longer, almost as if an understanding passed between them.

"Thanks for ... thanks for meeting me. Have a great day," she said.

Geret smiled and nodded as Lacey turned and walked away.

Lacey's thoughts were racing by the time she reached her office. She sat down in her chair and exhaled. She just stared at the wall for a few minutes trying to figure out what had just happened. Geret was Mr. Rude, except that he was definitely not rude. It had taken major willpower for her to remain composed in his presence. He had an effect on her, unlike any she had experienced before. Even George had not caused this kind of reaction to stir in her. Lacey shook her head as she sat in her office chair as if she were trying to shake off the feeling.

She looked at the time. It was only nine o'clock. She exhaled loudly as she resigned herself to get started on the paperwork. She picked up the patient chart off the top of the stack on her desk and reviewed the lab results. Then she began to review patient phone call messages since she didn't have to see patients until later in the morning. She found that she was having trouble concentrating.

Barbie stuck her head in the doorway, leaning one hand on the knob. "Hey Dr. B, how are ya?"

Lacey looked up at her without saying anything.

"Are you okay, Dr. Bartlett? You seem a little lost in thought," Barbie commented.

Lacey smiled and then motioned toward a chair. "I'm fine. Come on in and have a seat."

Barbie's facial expression turned to concern as she looked at Lacey with wide eyes. "Is everything okay?" She asked, taking a seat in the chair.

"Everything is fine. I just thought we could catch up for a minute," Lacey said.

"Okay. Cool. So, how has your morning been? Didn't ya have a meeting earlier this morning?" Barbie asked.

"Yes, I met with Geret Blake to talk about my instruments. He was very nice," Lacey replied, hoping Geret's name might cause Barbie to tell her a little about him.

Barbie flashed a wide smile, showing her braces and replied, "He's super nice and super cute. Now, he would be the perfect guy for you, Dr. B."

Lacey looked down at a chart and nonchalantly asked, "What's his story?"

Barbie shook her head and said, "Well, he's pretty tight-lipped about his past, but there are rumors. The story is that he moved here from California to play college football at Idaho State University. His girlfriend ... I think her name was Darla ... she stayed behind in California. She was in college there and was the cheer captain for the cheer team. Then she went on to be a Los Angeles Lakers' dancer on their dance team." Barbie paused and asked, "You know, the NBA team?"

Lacey nodded.

Barbie continued, "After college, Geret had planned to move back to California to be with Darla, but she ran off with one of the pro players. So Geret decided to stay here. I was told that Darla tried to get back together with Geret. When he wouldn't take her back, she thought she could buy her way back into his heart. Her family has a lot of money. But Geret still wouldn't have her. Then she tried to ruin him by slandering him, but no one believed her. Everyone who knows Geret knows he's a solid guy. He has a good heart, and he's one of those guys that is the definition of integrity."

Lacey felt a twinge of excitement that Geret wasn't married, but she also felt self-conscious knowing he had dated a Lakers' dancer. Then she wondered why she even cared. She said, "Wow, that's quite a story. He's kind of like a celebrity then, right?"

Barbie chuckled, "Exactly. He's had his dirty laundry smeared all over the town." Then her affect changed to disdain, and she said, "I feel sorry for him, though. He's such a good guy, and he didn't deserve all of that negative gossip. I think Darla burned him pretty bad. I don't think he's dated anyone since that mess. I'm telling ya, Dr. B, I can see the two of you as a couple."

Lacey's heart unexpectedly jumped at that thought. She gave Barbie a smile, nod, and roll of the eyes and asked, "Is that so?"

Barbie raised her eyebrows and smiled and then disappeared into the hallway.

Lacey sat back and tried to absorb Geret's story. If the story was true, Geret had been cheated on. Her heart ached for his pain, but she wasn't sure why she felt so attached to him. Perhaps it was the shared broken spirit they had both experienced. She and Geret had both been hurt by someone they cared for deeply. She could empathize with his loss.

Chapter Twelve

Lacey was on call the following weekend. Thankfully, the patient phone call volume was light. She only received a few calls from women who thought they might be in labor, but once they had come into the hospital, their contractions had gone away. So, Lacey was able to send them home due to false labor.

On Saturday morning, Lacey performed a scheduled Cesarean section. Geret happened to be on call that day, and he was the circulating nurse during the surgery. Right at the end of the procedure, the patient started to hemorrhage. Lacey was thankful Geret had been there because he was quickly able to get Lacey the medications she needed for the patient. He had even gone down to the blood bank to retrieve the packed red blood cells the patient needed for transfusion. He had been so responsive, and Lacey could see him putting his heart into patient care. She couldn't help but be impressed with his dedication to his work.

After the surgery, Lacey sat in the recovery room typing in orders for the patient's postoperative care. She had also decided to stay close by for a while to be sure the patient wouldn't have another bleed. As she typed in orders, she glanced up momentarily. She happened to catch the recovery room nurse interacting with Geret. He was talking to the nurse about the patient. Clearly, the young, cute, blonde nurse had someone other than the patient on her agenda. She was obviously flirting with Geret as she giggled and twirled her hair with her finger.

Lacey just stared at them. On the one hand, she was not happy to see a nurse flirting with another nurse in the workplace when a sick patient needed their undivided attention. On the other hand, she felt a heaviness in her gut that another woman was flirting with Geret.

Lacey looked back at the screen and began typing again. *Why am I feeling jealous?*

Geret walked away momentarily and then returned with some blankets in his arms.

Lacey couldn't help but stare at his arms. They were big, muscular, and sculpted. She allowed her stare to linger a moment too long as Geret looked up from the patient to her and smiled.

Lacey felt a flush come to her cheeks, and she diverted her attention back to the computer screen. *Busted*, she thought. She didn't want him to think she was staring at him, so she stood from her chair and walked over to him. "Thank you so much for your help today. I appreciate how quickly you took care of my patient's medications. And thanks for running to the blood bank."

Geret smiled his big smile and responded humbly, "You're welcome. That's what I'm here for." His eyes locked with hers briefly.

She thought she could see a sadness in his eyes, again, just like the first time she had looked in his eyes. This time it was undeniable, and she found herself wanting to know more about him.

At eleven-thirty that night, Lacey drove home in the dark. Snow was falling lightly. As an obstetrician, she had become accustomed to being up at any and all hours of the night. Eventually, the lack of sleep would start to wear on her after a few days if she didn't get adequate rest. Tonight, she had expected to be tired, but she wasn't. She pulled her SUV under the carport at the side of the house and turned off the engine.

In the kitchen, she warmed up a leftover chicken breast and green beans from the night before and then gulped her dinner down. She hadn't realized how hungry she was. After her meal, she hugged her arms and felt goosebumps. There was the usual chill in the air.

She walked into the living room, flipped on the fireplace switch, and sat on the hearth for a few minutes to warm up. She had an uneasy, empty feeling as she looked around her quiet house. She felt lonely.

Lacey walked back into the kitchen and filled the tea kettle with water. She put it on the gas stove top and set the flame to high. She pulled a mug from the cabinet and placed a tea bag in it. When the water was hot on the stove, she turned it off and filled the mug with steaming, hot water. She stood there leaning over the counter as the tea bag steeped.

She looked around the kitchen. She could imagine her grandmother, Vivian, standing there cooking a meal or steeping hot tea. She could imagine her grandfather, Joseph, sitting at the kitchen table reading a newspaper, occasionally looking up to comment on what Vivian was saying. Lacey imagined that Vivian and Joseph had hosted many dinner parties in this house. She peered through the opening over the bar into the dining room. The room was elegant, with its large crystal chandelier and wall sconces. She could imagine the room full of people and could hear their conversation and laughter. The dining room set was the only furniture left in the house that had belonged to her grandparents.

Lacey carried her tea into the dining room through a swinging door by the kitchen entrance. She sat down in the seat at the head of the table. The table was made of oak and was long. It could easily seat ten people. Lacey ran her hand over the surface of the table. It was worn and aged from the years. As she ran her hand over the grooves in the table, she had the sudden feeling of déjà vu, as if she had been here before.

Lacey stood and carried her tea to the bedroom. She opened the top drawer of her dresser and took out a box. It was a small, light-weight wood box with a lid. She had decorated this box as a young child and had kept important photographs and trinkets in it. She carried the box over to her bedside and set her tea down on the bedside table. Sitting Indian-style on the bed, she leaned up against a pillow against the headboard. She took the lid off the box and pulled out a stack of photographs.

She sorted through several photographs until she found the one she was looking for. The photograph showed a picture of Lacey on her first birthday. She was seated in a high chair at the end of the old, oak dining room table. The high chair food tray had been removed, and the chair was pushed up against the end of the table. Her father was kneeling beside her in the picture. He was wearing a paper birthday hat, strapped under his chin. He was smiling, and his eyes seemed to beam with happiness. Lacey turned the photograph over. On the back were the handwritten words, "My Lacey Lou, May 31, 1981." Lacey looked through all of the photographs, and she recognized different parts of the house in various pictures. Somehow, living in the house now made her feel closer to her family from years ago. *I wish I could remember more, Daddy*, she thought.

As Lacey returned the photographs to the box, something in a photograph caught her eye. The picture showed Lacey, as a toddler, standing in front of a tall wardrobe. Lacey looked up. Directly across from the foot of her bed was a built-in wardrobe. It wasn't the same color as the one in the photograph, but Lacey surmised that it had been painted. She stood and walked over to it. She compared the wardrobe to the photograph. It was the same one. Up until now, Lacey hadn't paid much attention to the wardrobe. She found it to be a beautiful addition to the room, but she considered it to be more of an antique. A closet had been added to the bedroom at some point in the last several years, so Lacey had not needed to use the built-in wardrobe. In fact, she had walked by it many times without giving it a second thought.

Lacey reached toward it and opened the swinging doors. It appeared to be empty. There was a hanging pole at the top and then a few drawers at the bottom. She opened the drawers and found that they were empty. She closed the swinging doors and then glanced at the base of the wardrobe. There were two more drawers. She opened the top one, which was empty. When she opened the bottom drawer, she was surprised to find a cardboard box. It was the size of a small moving box, and it was closed and sealed with packing tape. The box appeared aged. On one side, Lacey could make out a handwritten name in ink. It read, "Dennis."

Chapter Thirteen

Geret sat back in his kitchen chair and exhaled. The spaghetti leftovers from the night before had hit the spot. He had come home from the hospital feeling ravenously hungry. The day had been long for a Saturday. What had started out as a scheduled, elective C-section had turned into a stressful, life-threatening situation for Dr. Bartlett's patient. The surgery had been going well up until the patient was being moved out of the operating room. Then, suddenly, the patient started to hemorrhage. Geret had to admit that Dr. Bartlett kept her cool and handled the emergency well.

There is something about her, he thought. Over the past few months, Geret had found himself wondering about Lacey Bartlett. She had made an impression on him from the first day she came into his office to discuss her surgery preferences. *But why has she made such an impression?* Geret thought to himself as he exhaled. For one, she was organized, even to the point of being a little OCD. He liked that about her because it made her a good doctor. She also knew what she wanted when it came to surgical instruments. Plus, she could command a stressful situation while giving precise orders. *It makes her easy to work with. I know what to expect,* he thought.

Geret shook his head. He wasn't sure why he wanted to know what made her tick. He had sworn off women. Darla caused some major damage to his heart, and he wasn't going to risk any further damage. Darla had been such an important part of his life. He had trusted her and had opened his heart to her. He almost married her. Yet, she didn't even have the nerve to call off their engagement before running off with another guy. He grimaced as he remembered the shock and embarrassment of finding out about her affair in the tabloids. There it was, on that cold December morning, on the front of page of *People's Biz* newspaper, right before Christmas, that picture of Darla with the Lakers' point guard, Reese Struthers. The headline read, "Reese's New Fling."

Geret didn't want to think about it anymore. Fatigue was overtaking him. He leaned forward with his elbows on the table and rubbed his eyes. The house felt quiet and cold. There was an uneasiness in his stomach, and he didn't want to admit that he was lonely. He stood up and walked to the living room, hoping to shake off the uneasy feeling. The fire in the wood burning stove needed attention, so he threw in another log. After sitting down in his armchair, he leaned forward toward the fire trying to warm himself. He looked out the window and could see the snow cover in the back yard under the back-porch light. It had been dark for some time. He glanced down at his watch to see that it was just past midnight.

Geret moved into the small subdivision of Surprise Valley after he had found out about Darla's affair. He had originally planned to return to Los Angeles and settle down with her in her high-rise condo after graduation from nursing school. That obviously hadn't gone as planned. He recalled Darla showing up at his house right after he moved in. It still made him angry. She came to his door, crying. She apologized for the affair and told him she hadn't "been thinking right." *No, she had definitely been thinking wrong,* he thought. She even bought an expensive home in LA and tried to bribe him to start a new life with her.

He had really loved her, though, and it had been hard to turn her away. *But I would do it again*, he thought. Still, the recollection pained his heart. Darla really turned his heart inside out. Even now, he wasn't sure he could ever trust another woman.

Then his thoughts turned to Lacey again. There was just something in her eyes. Aside from the sadness he saw, there was kindness and sincerity. She didn't wear loneliness outwardly, but he could sense it in her demeanor. She was beautiful, too, with her green eyes, long brown hair, and petite build. The woman's looks alone begged for a charming man to care for her and treat her well. She appeared to have a tough exterior, but he sensed that she needed someone to care for her. He didn't know what her story was, but he wanted to know more. He closed his eyes and laid his head in his hands. He prayed, *Lord, you are the only one who knows the heart. Please bring someone into my life who won't break mine. Show me if there is a place for Lacey Bartlett in my life.*

Chapter Fourteen

Lacey pulled back the packing tape from the box. She could feel her heart race with excitement and anticipation, knowing that the contents of this box might have belonged to her father. She cautioned herself, as she pulled open the top flaps of the box, realizing that she might not find anything of substance. Her heart desperately wanted to know more about her heritage, her grandparents, and her father.

At first, Lacey could only see crumpled newspaper in the box. She removed several pieces, dropping them on the bed until she came to the first item in the box. She reached in and pulled out a tiny pair of Kinney white baby shoes. She studied them, wondering if they might have been hers. The white shoes had several scuff marks on the toes, and the strings were a dingy color. She looked inside the shoe and could see they were size three and a half. She exhaled softly at the thought that perhaps she had once worn them.

She placed the shoes on her bed and reached in the box and pulled out a silver baby cup. It was tarnished, but she could still see the ornate heart on one side and the initials LEB, her initials, on the other side. She looked at the bottom of the cup, and it read "Reed & Barton." Lacey placed the cup on the bed next to the shoes.

The next item she pulled from the box was a baby blanket. It was light pink and crocheted. Lacey carefully opened the blanket, and another matching blanket fell out onto the floor, except that it was light blue. Lacey picked up the blue blanket and opened it to find two pairs of crocheted booties in pink and blue tucked inside. She had to admit that she was confused about the blue blanket and booties. Blue was the classic color for baby boys. She picked them up and gently placed them on the bed. Then she carefully folded the blankets and held them to her chest. She closed her eyes as tears erupted. She imagined her mother and father holding her in these blankets at one time. If only she could be that close to her parents again.

Lacey sat on the bed for a while, clutching the blankets next to her heart. She felt sadness and loss. She wanted to belong with someone, somewhere; yet this house, these few items, and her limited memories were all she had of a family. She began to cry as the reality of her loss sank in. She had also been abandoned by the three men in her life that she had loved. Marco hadn't been able to honor his commitment of marriage, Jack hadn't loved her enough, and George just hadn't loved her.

After some time, Lacey yawned and realized how tired she was. It was after one o'clock in the morning. She reached into the box one last time. She initially thought she had only felt the bottom of the box, but her fingers slid along the edge of something linear. It felt like it might be a book.

She peered into the box and grasped the edges of the item and lifted it. She held it up. It was a large hardback book, but it was thin. She turned it over to see the words, "Walt Disney Presents Little Red Riding Hood." There was a picture of Little Red Riding Hood walking on a forest path carrying a basket of goodies. Further down the path, the big bad wolf was hiding behind a tree. Then a little further down the path was grandmother's house. Lacey opened the hardcover to the first page, and within the cover was a large record. She couldn't remember the exact size of the record, but by its size, she knew it was old.

Suddenly, she realized that she had seen this storybook and record before. Lacey gasped. She remembered this. She couldn't believe it, but she could remember sitting in her father's lap while the record was playing and could faintly recall turning the pages of the book with her father. Lacey sat down on the bed and read through the story page by page. She closed her eyes at the end of the story and sat in silence for a long time. The memory was vague, but it was wonderful. She cherished having any memory of being with her father. "I wish I could have known you, Daddy," she whispered.

After a while, Lacey stood up and gently placed the items back in the box. Then she carefully placed the box back inside the wardrobe drawer. She was exhausted. She changed into her pajamas, brushed her teeth, and then crawled into bed. As she was falling asleep, she prayed, *Thank you for these memories, Lord. Please, give me a family to love.*

Chapter Fifteen

As the month of December went by, Lacey's office and surgery schedule became packed with patients. By Friday of the week before Christmas, Lacey was exhausted. Despite her exhaustion, she looked forward to coming to the office every day. Barbie had decorated the office for the cheerful holiday. The Christmas tree in the waiting room had a breast cancer theme. It was decorated with pink and white twinkle lights, white garland, pink ribbons, and several shiny, silver ornaments. The patients had been encouraged to decorate and hang pre-cut paper ornaments on the tree. They could write in the name of a loved one who had been affected by breast cancer. The tree was festive and comforting. The rest of the waiting area was decorated with ornaments, twinkling lights, and garland. Christmas music played throughout the day in the waiting room and common patient areas. Lacey loved this time of year. She was mesmerized by the view of the snow-capped mountains and the steady, falling snow. It was freezing cold outside, but the holiday cheer and beautiful scenery gave the season a warm and cozy feel.

Lacey sat at her desk and paused after she finished her charts.

Her thoughts were interrupted as Barbie popped her head in the door. "Dr. Bartlett, it's time for the Christmas party. Are ya coming? We can walk over together."

Lacey looked up from her charts. "I wouldn't miss it," she said as she stood up, grabbed a wrapped present, and headed to the door. The party was held in the clinic lobby. The lobby was large and open with high ceilings. The windows and stairwell were decorated with twinkle lights, evergreen garland, and large candy canes. There was a tall twelve-foot Christmas tree decorated with white twinkle lights and large, shiny ornaments in shades of red, green, and white.

Several tables had been set up and were covered with festive table cloths lined with glittery snowflake designs and multi-colored twinkle lights. A buffet-style dinner was served on a few tables, and there were two dessert tables. Behind the tables was an open bar. Servers brought around hors d'oeuvres and glasses of wine. A local band was playing live music as a singer belted out Christmas songs one after another. This party was quite the setup and not what Lacey had expected. All of the physicians and employees of the clinic and hospital were invited.

Lacey felt a little out of place since she didn't know many people yet. The individual offices had drawn names for gift-giving, so there was a lot of cheer heard around the room as gifts were exchanged and unwrapped. There were several squeals of delight and hugs all around. Barbie and Lacey spent a few moments together exchanging and opening gifts, and then Barbie was whisked away in a conversation.

Since Lacey wasn't on call, she decided to sip on a glass of red wine to calm her nerves. She stood alone and glanced around the room. Barbie was working the crowd easily as she went from person to person. She was laughing and joking and knew everyone by name. Lacey walked over and stood by the window to glance out at the night sky. The moonlight shone on the snow caps, and Lacey couldn't help but exhale.

"Excuse me," said a voice from behind her, "Are you the new OB doctor in town?"

Lacey turned toward the voice and looked up to see a tall, broad-shouldered man with black hair and light brown eyes. "Yes, I am," she said, smiling at him.

"Hi, I'm Rusty Simms," he said, reaching to shake her hand. He was smiling, and his eyes had a glazed-over look to them as if he had been drinking a little too much. He was attractive and looked festive, dressed in a white shirt and a Santa tie. Covering part of his black hair was a Santa hat.

"It's nice to meet you," she said.

"I'm one of the anesthesiologists here," he said.

Lacey seemed puzzled, and she furrowed her brows. She thought she had met all of the anesthesiologists since she worked closely with them in surgery. She said, "Well, I guess I haven't worked with you in surgery yet."

He smiled with a sly expression, raised an eyebrow, and said, "I don't do that kind of work anymore. I'm a pain medicine specialist. I have my own pain clinic."

Lacey raised her eyebrows and nodded at hearing this. She said, "Well, that explains why we haven't met then."

Rusty's movements seemed slow, and Lacey could tell he was concentrating to keep his speech steady. She wondered how many glasses of wine he had consumed already. Just as she had formed that thought, Rusty leaned in toward her and lost his footing. He bumped her slightly and righted himself slowly.

"Sorry," he said. Then, as if nothing had happened, he asked, "So, when can I show you around town? I heard that you're here alone, and a lovely lady like yourself needs company." He just stood there grinning at her, swaying a little.

Lacey stared at him cautiously, not sure how to respond.

"Hey, Dr. Bartlett," came a voice from behind Lacey.

Lacey turned to see Geret. She was grateful for his interruption.

Before Lacey could respond, Geret asked, "May I borrow you for a second? I need to go over some things with you for Monday's case." Geret appeared to be cautiously glancing between her and Rusty.

"Hey, this is a party," Rusty blurted out. He added, "There will be no business tonight."

Lacey smiled at Geret, and then she turned toward Rusty, and said, "Actually, I asked Geret to find me because I wanted to talk about this case. Nice talking to you, Rusty." Then she walked off with Geret.

Rusty stood there for a moment, unsure of what had happened. He had an irritated look on his face. Then, as if he'd forgotten why he was standing there, he swaggered off to find another drink.

Lacey followed Geret to a corner of the room. She looked at him, wide-eyed, and smiled. "Thank you so much for rescuing me. That Dr. Simms is quite the character. I think he's had a little too much to drink tonight."

Geret nodded and smiled. He said, "I've been watching him tonight. He has a reputation for drinking too much at parties, even work parties. I figured it was only a matter of time and number of downed drinks before he made his way to you."

Lacey tilted her head to one side and smiled. She replied, "Thanks for looking out for me."

Geret seemed a little embarrassed and said, "Well, he usually singles out the most attractive women. I'm sure he asked you out, right?"

Lacey was pleased to hear Geret include her in the "attractive woman" group. Then she furrowed her eyebrows and replied, "I think he did." She smiled at Geret playfully.

They both laughed.

"So, are you enjoying yourself?" He asked.

Lacey exhaled and replied, "Honestly, I'm not a social butterfly. I don't like these kinds of events unless I'm with close friends. All of my close friends are scattered around the country practicing medicine, so I'd rather be at home right now."

"Where are your friends?" Geret asked.

Lacey smiled at the thought of her friends. She said, "Well, my two best friends from medical school are the ones I keep up with, mostly by text. Jen is a Pediatrician and lives in Jacksonville, Florida. Katy is an Ophthalmologist and lives in San Diego." Then she sighed and stared off into the distance and added, "They both have families and full lives."

"Your life isn't full?" He asked.

Upon hearing that question, Lacey looked at Geret. She hadn't meant to say that. She searched his face for a deeper question behind his first one. Then she answered, "I just meant that they are very busy managing work and family life."

He smiled cautiously as if he wanted to take the question back. "I'm sorry, I didn't mean to get personal."

Lacey shook her head saying, "No, it's fine. No worries."

There was an awkward silence between them as they glanced at each other. Then, to change the subject, Lacey asked, "Can you recommend a good plumber?"

Geret seemed to relax at the change of subject. He hadn't wanted to offend her. He smiled and said, "I can help you. What kind of problem are you having?"

Lacey was confused and asked, "You can help me with a plumbing problem?"

He smiled his wide smile, and Lacey could see the dimples in his cheeks. He replied, "Yes, I actually worked as a plumber when I was in nursing school. I'm pretty cheap, too."

Lacey felt more at ease now. She said, "Well, my old farmhouse kitchen faucet has been leaking since I moved in. I think it's getting worse."

"Easy fix," he said. "Will you be home tomorrow?"

"Yes, I'm off tomorrow," Lacey replied.

"I'm off, too. What time do you want me to come by?" He asked.

"Really, you don't mind?" She asked, wrinkling her forehead.

"Not at all. A dripping faucet will make you crazy after a while. I'll have it fixed in no time," he said.

Lacey smiled and shrugged her shoulders. She said, "Okay, if you're sure. How about ten o'clock?"

"I'll be there at ten," he replied.

Lacey was surprised by his offer to help her. He hardly knew her. Tonight, he had rescued her from Rusty and offered to fix her plumbing problem. She wasn't sure why, but his willingness to help her made her feel excited and cautious at the same time. "Well, great then. Thank you. I'm going to head home," she said.

"Drive safely," he said with a genuine look of concern in his eyes.

"Thanks, you too," she replied as she waved and walked off.

Chapter Sixteen

On Saturday morning, Lacey awoke at eight o'clock. She spent an hour sipping her coffee while reading her Bible devotionals. Unhurried mornings like these were welcome since she had so few of them. She wondered how long she would be able to keep up her current pace at the hospital. The pace at the office had been set on full-speed from the first day of her practice, and she had hoped it would have slowed by now. On top of the fast pace and packed office, she had to treat many high-risk pregnancies. Not only had the physical fatigue become a factor for her, but also the mental stress was beginning to contribute to her feelings of exhaustion.

She sighed as she glanced out the picture window from her couch. The snow was falling peacefully. She looked at her cell phone for the time. It was nine o'clock. Geret would be over at ten. His name rang as a pleasant sound in her thoughts. His face flashed in her mind. She smiled as she recalled his smile and dimples. He was definitely easy on the eyes. The idea of being on a date with him entered her mind for a moment. *I think I would really like that*, she thought. *But he would eventually find some reason he didn't want to be with me.* Then again, it didn't matter. She didn't want to date someone she worked with. *Too complicated.* She was just happy at the thought of noticing someone other than George. Only a few months previously, her heart had been so broken over George. *I guess this is progress*, she thought.

Lacey stood from the couch and walked over to the window, wanting to change the conversation in her head. Her self-doubt was evident. She couldn't help it, based on the fact that the three men she had loved had somehow each lost interest in her. They had all professed or implied love for her, but none of them were here with her now. *What's wrong with me?* She thought. She felt despair creeping in. "No," she said out loud, "I am worthy of love." She prayed, *Lord, give me strength. Remind me who I am to you. I know that what you think is really all that matters. I know you love me, and you've promised you'll never leave me.*

Lacey's mother had taught her to always cling to God's promises. Lacey knew that when she started to feel down, hopeless, or sad, she needed to remember God's promises written in the Bible. At this moment, she remembered Isaiah 41:10. It seemed to be her most quoted verse over the past six months. She would not be afraid because she knew God was with her and would strengthen her. Lacey took a deep breath. She turned and walked back into the kitchen to put her coffee cup in the sink. Then she headed to her bedroom to get dressed.

At ten o'clock, Lacey heard a knock at the front door. She opened the door to find Geret standing there with the wind whipping snow all around him.

"Good morning," Geret said.

"Hi. Come on in. It's freezing out there," she said, stepping aside to let him in. She closed the door quickly to avoid any more snow being blown in with the cold wind.

Geret stomped his feet on the entry rug, and "Thanks." Inside the foyer, Geret took off his boots and set them near the front door.

Lacey stepped into the living room to move out of his way. Then she said, "Follow me. I'll take you to the kitchen."

Geret followed Lacey down the hallway into the kitchen and said, "This place is really cozy. When was it built?"

Lacey replied, "In the 1940s. My grandparents bought it when they married in 1950, a few years before my dad was born. It's pretty old, but it's been maintained well and has had several upgrades."

In the kitchen, Geret took his coat off and hung it on a kitchen chair. He glanced around and said, "Wow, there is a lot of history in this house."

Lacey smiled at him and replied, "Yes, I just wish I knew more of it. I lived here with my parents and grandparents until I was two or three."

Geret asked, "Is that when you moved to Kentucky?"

"Yes, my mother and I moved to Louisville to be closer to her parents after my dad passed away," Lacey replied.

Geret's eyes conveyed his empathy, and he said, "I'm so sorry about your dad. I remember you told me that the first day I met you."

Lacey said, "It's okay. Like I said, I don't even remember him. I mean, I have some faint memories, but I was so young when he died."

"So, is it just you and your mom now?" He asked.

Lacey exhaled looking off into the distance. She replied, "No, my mother passed away about fifteen years ago from breast cancer."

"I'm sorry. I think I already knew that. You told me that the first day I met you, too. I feel like I need to remove my foot from my mouth. I have asked only insensitive questions this morning," said Geret.

Lacey shook her head and smiled. She said, "No, you're fine. You were just asking normal questions."

He smiled at her and then he asked, "How about this question? Do you happen to have a toolbox?" He looked over at the faucet as he spoke. "I brought some tools I thought I would need, but I actually need something else."

Lacey thought for a minute. Then she remembered something. She said, "I'm not sure, but I know I saw a toolbox out in the garage. I don't know what's in it, but you may find what you're looking for there."

Geret glanced out the window and could see the garage. He asked, "Is it locked?"

Lacey answered, "No, there is nothing of value in there. I don't lock it. The toolbox is sitting on a wooden bookshelf. You can't miss it."

Geret grabbed his coat and turned toward the kitchen entrance and said, "Okay, I'll go get my boots on and go out the front door. I'll be right back."

Ten minutes passed, and Geret returned through the front door. He removed his boots again and then wandered back into the hallway on his way to the kitchen. He could smell the fresh aroma of coffee brewing.

Lacey was seated at the kitchen table sipping a cup of coffee when Geret walked through the kitchen entrance. "Did you find what you were looking for?" She asked.

Geret nodded and said, "Yes, I did. I also found something else I thought you might want to see." He reached out to Lacey and handed her a small, brown, leather-bound book. "It's a Bible."

Lacey took the Bible and laid it on the table. "Thanks," she said. "Where did you find it?"

"It was in the toolbox," Geret replied.

Lacey opened the Bible. Inside the front cover, there was a handwritten inscription. It read:

To our son, Dennis Joseph Bartlett,

Love, Dad and Mom, December 25, 1965.

Lacey thought for a minute. *Dad would have been ten in 1965. He must have received this for Christmas that year.*

Geret looked up from his work on the faucet. He asked, "Any clues as to whom it belonged to?"

Lacey looked up at Geret and smiled. She said, "Yes, it was my father's Bible. It looks like this was a Christmas gift to him from my grandparents when he was ten." She thumbed through the Bible gently. There were several underlined passages and notes in the margins on various pages.

Lacey didn't realize she was holding her breath and staring at the Bible until she heard Geret ask, "Are you okay?"

"Yes, sorry. I just can't believe you found this," she replied.

Geret could see she was holding back tears. He had completed his task, so he changed the subject. He said, "Good as new."

"What?" Lacey asked, confused.

Geret smiled at her. "The faucet is fixed. No more dripping."

"Oh," Lacey said, exhaling, "Thank you so much. That didn't take you long."

"Easy fix," he replied. Geret started to gather his things and put his coat back on.

Lacey asked, "Do you want a cup of coffee? I just brewed a fresh pot."

Geret smiled again, and replied, "No, I wish I could, but I have to get going. I need to shovel my driveway and go get some firewood."

Lacey felt the feeling of rejection creeping in. *Not that it matters since I'm not going to date a guy from work*, she reminded herself. Still, it bummed her out that he didn't want to stay for a cup of coffee. He really was here just to fix the faucet.

"Oh, okay," Lacey replied. Then she asked, "You have a wood-burning fireplace? I haven't seen one of those for years."

"Yes, well, it's a wood-burning stove, and I like getting heat the old-fashioned way," he replied, playfully. "You can come sit by it for warmth sometime. It's definitely cozy." Then he winked at her.

Lacey couldn't help but smile. She felt a surge of warmth and a hint of flirtation in his words. *Was he just flirting?* Whatever it was, she liked it.

Geret started to walk down the hallway toward the front door. Lacey followed him. Geret bent down to put his boots on, and he said, "I hope you're able to find some good memories in that Bible I found. I have a feeling you will." Then he stood up and placed his hand on the doorknob. He turned to look at her one last time and said, "God speaks to us in many different ways."

Lacey felt her heart jump at the tenderness in his words. She felt comfort. Without thinking, she embraced him. For a moment, he seemed surprised at her intrusion into his space. But within a second, she felt him hug her back. After a moment, she stepped back, feeling embarrassed. She had no idea where that bold move had come from.

Lacey could feel her face flush. She put her hands to her cheeks and said, "Thank you for fixing my faucet, and thank you for finding my father's Bible. It means a lot to me."

"You're welcome. I'm glad to help anytime," he said.

Lacey smiled at him saying, "Be safe."

Then he disappeared behind the closing door. Geret stood against the closed door for a few minutes. Lacey's embrace had given him a feeling of comfort that he hadn't felt in a long time. He couldn't remember the last time he had been that close to a woman. He liked holding her slender, petite frame in his arms. There was something soulfully familiar about her. She felt like home.

Chapter Seventeen

Lacey stared out the window in the living room watching Geret drive off in his blue truck. It had been nice to have a visitor. Other than a brief visit by Barbie once, she hadn't had any visitors until today. The house had felt a little less lonely with Geret's presence.

She started to feel flushed again as she recalled the hug. She wasn't sure what had possessed her to hug him, but she was glad she did it. It felt good to be close to him. She hadn't felt that kind of comfort for a long time.

Her mother had always commented about the importance of hugs. She had said, "People who get hugs live longer." *There must be something to that*, she thought. Being in Geret's arms for that brief moment breathed some life into her. She couldn't stop thinking about being pressed up against his big chest and engulfed in his muscular arms.

His words about the Bible seemed so insightful. He knew she was searching. It was as if he had seen a glimpse of her soul. She was searching for memories of her family, clues about her heritage, and who she was without them. She was trying to understand her reason for being here in this house at this time in her life.

Lacey walked back to the kitchen and sat down at the kitchen table. She slowly opened her father's Bible running her fingers over some of the notes in the margins. He must have used this as his Bible for most of his life. Some of the notes were printed and others were in cursive. She slowly flipped the pages through the Old Testament. As she flipped through Proverbs, she noticed a folded note in the first few pages.

Lacey carefully lifted the note. It was folded in fourths and appeared to be aged, yellow steno paper. She unfolded the paper and inside was a letter addressed to "Lacey Lou." Lacey felt her heart jump and start to race. She held her breath as she held up the note. At the top of the note, Proverbs 3:5 and 6 were handwritten. Lacey loved these Bible verses and had committed them to memory when she was a young girl. She read over the verses, and then she read her father's handwritten note.

My Dearest Lacey Lou,

Today, God brought you into our lives. This is both the happiest and saddest day of my life. I had to write down my feelings because I don't know what to do with my mixed emotions. You may never see this note, and it is probably for the best. Your mother and I wish to spare you from any pain in this life, if it is within our power.

You are such a beautiful baby. Luke is also perfect, though I can't stop the tears as I mention his name. You have the most beautiful skin and the sweetest smile. Luke is beautiful, too. I am so heartbroken that he didn't make it. Hannah was lost, too. She will never know either of you.

The doctors still are uncertain as to what happened. They called it a cord accident and said it must have just happened a few hours before you were both born.

I wrote this passage from Proverbs to remind myself that God is in control, and that no matter what happens, I will trust Him. I will pray every day that you grow up to become a successful, God-fearing, young woman. Somehow, knowing that you are always in His care gives me comfort.

I know Luke is with Him now, and I long for the day that I will see him again in heaven. My Lacey Lou, I promise that I will teach you to always trust God for everything, as I am having to trust Him now.

All my love,

Daddy

Lacey lay the note down on the open Bible. She could not believe what she had just read. Her thoughts were racing, and she could feel her anxiety building. *I had a brother?* According to this letter from her father, she had a twin brother who had died just before birth. Suddenly, the blue baby blanket and booties made sense. Her thoughts continued to race. *Why hadn't Mom told me about him? Why was Luke such a big secret? Did Mom think I wouldn't be able to handle this news? How could she have kept this from me? And who was Hannah?* She couldn't understand why her mother would have kept this from her. It didn't make any sense.

In her mother's last days, she and Lacey had spent almost every moment together. Her mother had given Lacey words of wisdom, important Bible verses to remember, and important life lessons. Not once had she mentioned her brother, Luke. Lacey felt frustrated. She wasn't angry with her because she knew her mother had her reasons for keeping this from her. There had to be something more.

Lacey folded the letter and tucked it back into the pages of Proverbs. She lay her head down on the table and rested her forehead on the closed Bible. She couldn't believe she had been born with a brother. She wanted to know more about what happened to Luke and why her mother never told her about him. Why had her father felt compelled to write her the letter? It was as if he knew he wouldn't live very long, and he wanted to make sure he had said certain things to Lacey. *But he died unexpectedly in a car accident.* None of it made sense. She prayed. *Lord, please give me wisdom. Help me to understand what happened to my brother and why you are revealing this to me now.*

Chapter Eighteen

On Monday, Lacey's surgery schedule was busy. Her first case was at seven o'clock. By one o'clock in the afternoon, she had performed five cases. Her fifth case had been challenging. The patient needed an abdominal hysterectomy due to a history of chronic pelvic pain. Because the patient had undergone several previous abdominal surgeries, she had extensive scar tissue. Lacey had to carefully dissect the scar tissue away from the healthy tissue, and this had been a long, tedious process. She was glad this was her last case of the day.

After the case, Lacey sat in the recovery room and typed orders into the computer. She had seen Geret a few times in passing throughout the morning, but she hadn't had a chance to talk to him. As she typed in the orders, she heard Geret's voice from behind her.

"Hey, Dr. Bartlett, how are you holding up today?"

Lacey turned to look at him, and said, "Honestly, I'm glad my cases are done." Geret was like a breath of fresh air. Lacey felt weary from standing for so long that morning, and her back was aching. Seeing Geret lifted her mood, and she couldn't help but smile at him. He smiled at her and seemed to be studying her face.

"Do you get a break now?" He asked.

"I think so. I'm on call tonight, but so far there is nothing urgent going on," she replied.

"You should go home and get something to eat and try to get a nap in," he said.

"You sound like a parent," she said, chuckling.

He looked at her more seriously, and said, "Someone has to take care of you."

Lacey didn't know what to say to that and remained speechless. She stared at him for a moment and then smiled. Finally, she said, "Thanks, but I'm fine."

Geret sat down across from her in a chair. He was sipping from a stainless-steel coffee thermos with the initials GLB carved into the side. He smiled at her, and said, "I've been wondering, did you look through your dad's Bible?"

Lacey was surprised at the change of subject. She didn't think he would care to remember it, but she hadn't stopped thinking about Luke or why her parents had kept him a secret from her. She replied, "Yes, I did."

"Did you find anything to help you on your quest?" He asked.

Lacey furrowed her eyebrows and asked, "My quest?"

"Yes," he said, "Your quest to know more about your family and heritage."

Lacey felt uncomfortable. She didn't want to discuss the letter here. She leaned in toward him and said quietly, "I did find something, but I'd rather not talk about it right now."

Geret seemed embarrassed. He said, "Oh, I'm sorry. I shouldn't have brought up such a sensitive subject here. I've just been thinking about you, and I wondered if you found anything. I'm sorry for the intrusion." Geret stood to leave.

Lacey could see that he had misunderstood her. She said, "What I meant to say is that I found something that I'd like to tell you about. You are the one who found the Bible for me, and I thought I'd share this information with you. I just thought I could show you what I found, maybe, over a cup of coffee?"

Geret's shoulders and face relaxed. He said, "Of course, I'd love that."

"Do you have plans for Friday night?" She asked.

He gave her a puzzled look and asked, "You know that's Christmas Day, right?"

"Oh, goodness. I forgot. I'm sorry. Why don't you let me know when you have time?" She replied, feeling like a loser. She had completely forgotten about Christmas since she didn't have any plans.

"Friday night is fine. I just wanted to make sure you didn't already have plans," he replied.

"Don't you have plans with your family?" She asked, furrowing her brows.

"No, I don't have any family," he replied.

Almost as if she didn't believe him, she asked, "What about your mom, dad, siblings, or even grandparents?"

He pursed his lips and shook his head replying, "Nobody. My grandparents passed away years ago. My dad left my mom when I was two, and my mom passed away from colon cancer three years ago. I'm an only child."

Lacey felt bad that she had never asked Geret about his family. She hadn't found the right time to ask him, and she hadn't wanted to come across as nosey when he was fixing her faucet. She said, "I'm sorry."

He smiled at her and said, "No worries. Looks like we are in the same boat. It will be nice to spend Christmas Day with someone this year."

Lacey smiled at his comment, and said, "Well, then it won't just be coffee. I'll make Christmas dinner for us."

"Sounds great," he replied.

As Geret turned to leave, she pointed to the initials on his thermos and asked him, "What does the 'L' stand for in your name?

Geret replied, "Luke."

Chapter Nineteen

Lacey was at home and had been sleeping for two hours when she received a call from Labor and Delivery.

"Hello?" Lacey answered with her sleepy voice.

"Hi, Dr. Bartlett. This is Veronica from Labor and Delivery. Two patients just arrived in early labor, and Dr. Dean has turned over his laboring patient to you. She is six centimeters dilated now."

Lacey exhaled and replied, "Okay, I'm on my way in."

Lacey disconnected the call and slowly rose from the couch. She walked into the kitchen to brew a small pot of coffee, then proceeded to the bathroom to freshen up. She had slept in her scrubs and a sweatshirt, so she only needed to put on her shoes and coat.

On her way out the door, she poured a thermos of hot coffee and added cream and sugar.

The wind was blowing hard as she walked to her SUV parked under the carport. Lacey sat inside her car sipping the hot coffee while the windows defrosted. She was thankful she had added seat warmers to her car at the time of purchase. Once her car was defrosted, she pulled onto the road.

Not only had there been snow every day in December, but high wind advisories had also been issued for truck drivers on the highways almost every day. Lacey had never heard of high wind warnings to truck drivers. In fact, a few semi-trucks had actually been blown over on the highway just the week before. She had only heard such loud, wind gusts during severe thunderstorms or tornadoes back East in the spring and summer, not in the winter months.

Lacey struggled to acclimate to the frigid climate. Although she lived close to the hospital, she was tired of going in and out of the cold, especially at night. The hospital provided rooms for doctors to stay in when they were on call and wanted to be close to their patients. During her drive, Lacey decided she would take up residence in one of those rooms tonight.

When Lacey arrived at Labor and Delivery, one of her patients was pushing, and the other one was nine centimeters dilated. Although the third patient belonged to Dr. Dean, he had turned over her care to Lacey. Since she was the on-call doctor, she was responsible for all of the patients. Lacey delivered the first patient's baby within fifteen minutes of her arrival, and then she had to deliver the second patient's baby by C-section. Dr. Dean's patient was now eight centimeters dilated, so Lacey retired to the call room to grab a few hours of sleep. The patient's progress in labor had been slow. She had refused an epidural and wasn't allowing the nurses to check her progress.

Just after midnight, Lacey received a call from Veronica, "Dr. Bartlett, the patient is screaming in pain, wanting to push, but she won't let me do an exam. The baby's heartbeat keeps dropping down to the sixties."

Lacey replied, "I'll be right there." Lacey walked down the hall to Labor and Delivery. Knowing that a normal fetal heart rate was between 120 and 160, Lacey was concerned about the baby's heart rate dropping into the sixties. She knew the baby would not be able to tolerate this pattern for long. She reviewed the fetal heart tracing and then spoke with the patient and her family before the patient finally agreed to an exam. The cervix was not completely dilated, and it was swollen from the patient pushing against it.

Lacey asked the patient to stop pushing, but she refused.

Lacey became concerned and said to the patient, "You have to stop pushing. Every time you push, the baby becomes stressed, and the heart rate falls."

The patient looked exhausted from pain. She cried out, "I can't stop pushing with the contractions. It hurts more if I don't push."

Lacey leaned in closer to the patient's face and said calmly, "If you don't stop pushing, the baby is going to be distressed to the point of needing a C-section."

The patient's next contraction started, and the patient screamed out, "I'm not having a C-section. I will push this baby out."

Lacey could tell the patient was pushing. The baby's heart rate dropped to thirty and stayed there. Two minutes passed without recovery of the baby's heart rate. Lacey could feel her own heart racing. She knew it was time to deliver the baby. She looked at the patient, and then she glanced to the patient's bedside at her husband and mother. She said, "I have to deliver this baby now." While Lacey spoke, she motioned to the nurses and said, "Call the anesthesiologist. We need to do a stat C-section." Lacey reached toward the monitors and unhooked them. Then she unlocked the bed and started to move the patient.

"I don't want a C-section!" The patient screamed out.

Lacey looked at the patient's husband and mother. Her husband said, "Dr. Bartlett, please do what you need to do."

Lacey had already started her plan in motion as she wheeled the patient toward the operating room.

In retrospect, Lacey was certain that God had put certain things in motion that night to help her. At this hospital, the general rule had been that the anesthesiologist did not have to be in the hospital unless a patient had an epidural or there was an active surgical case. Neither of these conditions existed at this time. However, the anesthesiologist happened to be in the hospital finishing up paperwork from the earlier C-section. When he heard what was happening, he met Lacey back in the operating room with the patient and put the patient to sleep within two minutes.

Chaos was the only way to describe the flurry of activity around Lacey. The nurses looked like little mice running to and fro, bumping into each other, and yelling for things. Lacey remained calm on the outside despite the erupting volcano inside of her. The whole thing seemed surreal, as if she were in a nightmare. She focused on her primary goal of getting the baby delivered and oxygenated. She knew the surgery team had been called in, but it could take up to thirty minutes for them to get there. That would be about twenty-eight minutes too late. The baby would die if she had to wait for them. Lacey had to act, now.

In this kind of emergent, surgical situation, the labor and delivery nurses had been trained to pull a specific instrument kit and lay out the instruments for the surgeon. From what Lacey could see, the nurses had found the kit, and one of the nurses was frantically laying out the instruments on a sterile table. *All I need is a scalpel*, Lacey told herself.

Lacey ran to the scrub sink and quickly scrubbed her arms and hands. Then she gowned and gloved herself. "No prep." She called out, and added, "Just splash her skin with betadine."

In normal, scheduled surgeries, the nurse would carefully apply a prep solution of iodine with a sponge to the area of skin being incised and the surrounding skin. But there was no time for that now, and Lacey knew a splash of betadine was better than nothing.

Lacey moved toward the table as she yelled out for the nurses to call the neonatologist to the delivery. She knew the baby would need resuscitation. Lacey moved to the patient's right side. There was no sterile drape in the kit, so Lacey held out her hand to get started.

"Scalpel," Lacey said.

Nothing happened.

Lacey looked up at the nurse who looked completely frazzled and said, "I can't find a blade handle. There isn't one in this kit."

The scalpel was composed of two parts, the blade and the handle. The nurse could not find a handle anywhere in the kit.

Lacey started to panic. She knew she was a good surgeon, but there was no way she could operate without a scalpel. Lacey looked to the other nurses and shouted, "Someone get me a scalpel!"

The nurses were frantically searching but coming up with nothing.

Lacey's heart began to sink as she looked at the patient lying on the surgery bed, asleep and intubated, with the distressed baby still in utero. Lacey's eyes started to tear up. She looked up and said, "Lord, help me." Almost instantly, her eyes drifted to the instrument table. There was no handle, but there was a blade. *All I need is a blade*, she realized.

She leaned over to the table and carefully grasped the small blade. She made a vertical midline skin incision on the patient's abdomen all the way down to the uterus. She then made an incision on the uterus and placed her hand around the baby's head. She pulled the baby's head gently to the incision and delivered the head and shoulders through the incision with ease.

The baby girl was lifeless. She was blue, not breathing and limp. Lacey looked up and yelled for the neonatologist, but in the excitement, someone had forgotten to call him. There was no time to waste. Lacey placed the baby on the patient's thighs since the baby was still attached to the umbilical cord. She would have to resuscitate the baby herself. She needed an Ambu bag and oxygen to ventilate the baby. She felt helpless, like a one-person operation.

She started yelling for someone to get an Ambu bag as she stared down at the blue baby girl. On the edge of desperation and feeling panicked, she looked up and almost screamed for help again. As she leaned down to give the baby mouth-to-mouth ventilation, she heard a voice.

"Here!"

Lacey looked up to see Geret moving toward her with an Ambu bag and mask. He seemed to come out of nowhere, like Superman. He immediately applied the mask and ventilated the baby.

Within thirty seconds, the baby had tone and good color and was crying vigorously. It was music to Lacey's ears. Lacey was shaking as she clamped and cut the umbilical cord. The neonatologist came into the room, and Lacey took the baby girl over to him at the warmer. She was going to be okay.

Lacey walked back to her patient, who was still asleep, intubated, and bleeding. Her heart was racing. She slowed her breathing down as she started to feel a little dizzy, and she knew she was hyperventilating. She looked up at Geret and asked, "Will you please get me a sterile drape and the rest of my instruments?"

"I'm already on it," he replied.

The mood in the operating room was still tense and quiet. Everyone was in shock and focused on completing necessary tasks. Lacey calmed herself and stayed on task. She delivered the placenta and sewed the patient's layers back together. The bleeding stopped. Lacey was reeling on the inside and knew that God had intervened for her. She exhaled with relief, knowing that both the mother and the baby were going to be okay.

Chapter Twenty

After the surgery, Lacey spoke to the patient's family. The fear in their eyes was evident when Lacey initially stepped into the waiting room. Lacey was grateful to God to be able to tell the patient's family that the patient and the baby were going to be okay. She could see the relief in the patient's husband's face. The patient's mother sobbed and hugged Lacey, thanking her over and over.

Instead of going to the recovery room, Lacey went directly into the locker room. Usually, after a surgery, she would go to the recovery room to complete her dictation and orders. But right now, she needed to recover. The locker room was quiet. The surgery team had gone home.

Lacey's emotions were in turmoil. She had felt terrified, panicked, uncertain, and helpless all rolled into one ball during the surgery. Now that the surgery was over, that ball of emotions in her heart and stomach threatened to erupt. And it did. Lacey went into the bathroom stall and slid to the ground onto her bottom. She planted her face in her hands, and the eruption occurred in the form of tears.

She couldn't even fathom the events that transpired. In her formal training, she had never encountered anything close to this. She had never been required to do a surgery without a scalpel. She had never been without the necessary resources and tools to perform surgery with confidence and precision. As a surgeon, she had never felt this scared. If even one part of that evening had been off at all, that baby would have died. This was truly a life or death situation, and she didn't like being this close to it.

The tears flowed mostly because Lacey felt scared. Not only did she feel fear, but she also felt alone. There was no one to comfort her, hold her, or tell her she would be okay. There was no one to talk to.

She raised her eyes to the ceiling. "Lord," she cried softly, "I'm tired. I'm lonely. I want to serve you, and I know you are with me. But Lord, I don't feel strong enough to be here alone. I was so afraid tonight. I don't want to be alone anymore."

Lacey was mostly referring to her current practice of high-risk patients. She was growing weary of taking on one emergency after another. But she was also referring to living alone. She felt desperately alone. She sat there for a few more minutes staring at the floor. Her life had been reduced to scary, sad, alone, and sitting on a dirty bathroom floor in a bathroom stall.

She was blowing her nose and wiping her tears when she heard a faint knock on the door to the bathroom. She quieted her sobs but didn't hear anything. Then she heard the knock again. "Is someone there?" she asked.

"It's Geret, Dr. Bartlett. Are you okay? Can I get you anything?" He asked softly.

Lacey gathered herself together, feeling a little embarrassed. She replied, "No, I'm fine, thanks. I'm about to head home."

Geret replied, "I know the night was rough. I just thought we could talk about it."

Lacey softly replied, "Thanks," but she couldn't get any other words out. She waited for Geret to reply, but he didn't.

She was relieved he hadn't seen her, though he had obviously heard her crying. It had been kind of him to come check on her, despite his awkward entrance into the ladies' room. She was thankful that he had shown up earlier that night to help her. She wanted to talk to him, but she couldn't right now. The emotions were overflowing, and she couldn't talk about any of it now. She needed to try and process it first, and she needed sleep.

Lacey collected her thoughts and wiped her face once again. She left the bathroom and pulled her purse and coat from her locker. Upon exiting the locker room, she found Geret sitting in the surgery lounge. Lacey felt embarrassed for him to see her flushed, swollen face, so she looked down at the floor. "Oh, I thought everyone had left," she said.

Geret stood, and he softly replied, "I'm going to stay behind until your patient leaves the recovery room. She is doing well." Geret's face was filled with empathy and understanding as his eyes met Lacey's.

Lacey gave him a nod and choked out, "Thanks." She was still on the verge of tears.

"I know you don't feel like talking about this now, but I hope you'll come talk to me when you're ready. You should have never been put in a situation where you didn't have the necessary resources. You saved that baby's life tonight," Geret said softly and poignantly.

Lacey lifted her eyes again from the floor to meet Geret's eyes. "Thank you for being there tonight to resuscitate the baby. I was feeling helpless when you walked in. You helped save her. I can't tell you how grateful I am." Lacey looked away as a tear rolled down her cheek.

Geret stood up and walked over to her. "I was scared too."

Lacey was leaning her hip on the table in the lounge with her hand resting on the table top. Geret could see she was shaking and placed his hand over hers. His hand was warm and strong. She felt a flutter in her stomach as her heart skipped a beat. His hand lingered for just a minute, and then he gently draped his arm around her shoulder and pulled her to him. She looked up at him and felt a little lightheaded as she took a deep breath.

"Hang in there, you really did a great thing tonight," Geret said as he removed his arm.

As awkward as this situation should have been, it wasn't. Lacey looked up at him, and for a moment, she just wanted to fall into his arms. She wanted to be held. He seemed to be searching her face as if he were trying to read her thoughts. She finally looked away and said quietly, "I'm going home. Thank you for everything. Have a good night."

Geret replied, "Goodnight. Be safe."

It was five o'clock that morning when Lacey finally arrived at home. She sent a text to Barbie that she would not be coming into the office that day and asked Barbie to reschedule her patients. She brushed her teeth and fell into bed, as was becoming her routine. The house was freezing, but she warmed up quickly under the covers. She closed her eyes and was comforted a little as she remembered the gentle touch and warmth of Geret's embrace.

Chapter Twenty-One

Lacey's cell phone chirped at noon. She opened her eyes uncertain of what the noise was. As she realized it was her phone, she turned toward her bedside table and reached for it.

She had a text message from Rusty. "I stopped by your office to see you this morning. Barb told me you weren't in today. I wanted to see if you were up for dinner tonight?"

Lacey exhaled a heavy sigh and rolled her eyes. She was so not interested in this man, but he couldn't take a hint. She begrudgingly texted back, "I had a rough call night last night. Had to reschedule patients. I'm too tired to go out. Thanks for asking."

Rusty texted back, "Well, when are you going to make time for me? I have a lot to show you around town. Maybe I can just cook for you. How would you like that? I'll stop over and prepare a meal for you."

Geez, he's pushy and desperate. Lacey knew he was considered attractive by all the single women in town. In fact, he had dated almost all of them. But she could see through this pompous act. She knew there wasn't much depth to his heart, and he had already turned her off by his drunken behavior at the Christmas party. She replied, trying to be as clear as possible, "Thank you for the offer, but I'm not interested." *There, that ought to be a clear message that I have no interest in him.*

Rusty's reply was one of a clueless man. He wrote, "Okay, we'll try another time soon."

Lacey closed her eyes and exhaled with frustration. She could feel her irritation growing when her cell phone rang. Thankfully, it was Barbie calling.

"Hello?" She said with a groggy voice.

"Dr. B, it's Barbie. Did I wake ya? I'm sorry," she said.

"No, I just woke up, Barbie. I need to get up anyway. How are you?" Lacey replied.

Barbie said, "I'm fine, but I'm worried about ya. It's not like ya to cancel office. Everybody has been talking about what happened last night. All of the doctors here at the practice are furious that the operating room didn't have a blade handle available. Did ya really deliver that baby with just a blade?"

Lacey rolled onto her back and then sat up. "Yes, I did. Wait, they're furious?"

Barbie replied, "Yeah, Dr. Dean was saying ya should have had all of the necessary instruments available. He is mad at the surgery staff. He has already had a meeting with Geret Blake today."

"Oh no," Lacey replied, "It wasn't anyone's fault." Lacey's thoughts started racing. Geret was the last person who should get in trouble for this.

"What happened anyway?" Barbie asked.

Lacey relayed the events of the previous night to Barbie.

"That's crazy, Dr. B. Sounds like Geret actually came to the rescue at the end," she said.

Lacey replied, "He did. I am grateful to him. I'm not blaming anyone. The surgical kit was missing a handle, or it fell out of the kit during the chaos. Whoever packs those kits just needs to have a checklist to make sure nothing is omitted. It all worked out; though, I admit, it was scary. I'm really shaken up over it. I was praying throughout the surgery. I know God helped me."

"Well, are ya okay?" Barbie asked.

"I didn't get home until five this morning. I was tired and emotionally drained," Lacey replied.

"I bet. I still can't believe that happened. I went ahead and rescheduled everybody," Barbie said.

"I'll be back in the office tomorrow. You can just add on patients as needed, and we'll have a long day," Lacey said.

"Ya have forty-two patients on tomorrow's schedule. So, yeah, it's going to be a long day. I tried to push a few appointments out, but your patients were adamant about seeing ya," Barbie said.

"That's fine. Thanks for doing that," Lacey replied.

"Dr. B, ya haven't really answered my question. Are ya really okay? I mean, do ya want me to stop by this afternoon? Do ya want some company?" Barbie asked.

"I'm okay, Barbie," Lacey replied. "I think I just need a little more rest."

"Okay, well, get some rest. If ya change your mind, I'll come right over," Barbie said.

"Thanks, Barbie. I'm so grateful for you. I'll see you tomorrow," Lacey replied.

Lacey disconnected the call. She looked down at her phone and saw that she had three missed calls from Dr. Dean. She dialed his number.

When he answered, he immediately asked, "Lacey, are you okay? I've been trying to reach you all morning. What happened last night?"

Lacey spent the next hour talking to him about the events from the night before. She made sure to applaud Geret for his help, and she made sure he knew that she didn't blame anyone.

After their discussion of the events, Dr. Dean said, "My patient and her family are indebted to you. They think that you hung the moon. The mom and baby are doing great. The patient's husband and mom said you just took command and took care of business."

Lacey pursed her lips and nodded. She replied, "Well, Stan, that's what we do, right? Besides, I had some divine help last night."

"You must have," he said.

"I did. I'm certain of it," Lacey said.

After Lacey disconnected the call, she could feel a headache coming on. She realized that the lack of caffeine was probably the culprit. "I need coffee," she said, as she rolled out of bed and put her slippers and robe on.

The house was cold as she stepped into the hallway. Instead of turning toward the kitchen, she walked into the living room and turned on the gas fireplace.

Lacey glanced around the living room as she warmed herself by the fire. Her Christmas tree was glistening in the sunlight from the window. She walked over to the tree and turned on its lights. The tree was pretty with its twinkle lights, garland, and sparkly ornaments. Lacey hadn't decorated the house this year because she hadn't had the time or energy. For a moment, she glanced at the space in front of the window where she had put the tree. She wondered if that's where her grandmother had put up her Christmas tree every year. Lacey exhaled, and then she headed to the kitchen for coffee.

She poured a cup and added cream and sugar and stood at the counter, lost in thought, as she took the first few sips. She was still reeling from the events the night before. Somehow that near-catastrophe had made her feel more alone. It was hard to manage one high-risk situation after another without being able to vent to someone about them.

She felt a deep longing to share her life with someone. Her thoughts turned to Geret. He had already shared several important moments with her, almost by default. He had come to her home and fixed her faucet. Then he had found her father's Bible. And last night he came to her rescue. He had even tried to comfort her. *Lord, are you trying to tell me something?*

Lacey shivered. She turned to walk toward the living room to sit near the fireplace. On the way, she stopped by her bedroom and retrieved her father's Bible from her bedside table.

In the living room, she nestled onto the couch and covered her legs with a blanket. She set her coffee down and opened the Bible. She removed the letter and read it again. Then she replaced it and continued to thumb through the rest of the Old Testament. She read through the various notes in the margins. There were some notations about specific verses and others that expressed his own thoughts. It was heartwarming to know that her father had enjoyed reading and studying the Bible.

When Lacey turned to the New Testament, the Bible opened to the book of Mark. Lacey's breath caught in her throat. There was another folded, yellow stenopaper. Lacey's breathing increased as she reached for the paper. *Is this another letter?*

She carefully unfolded the dated paper. It had been folded in fourths like the last one. When she unfolded the paper, she saw "My Dearest Lacey Lou" handwritten at the top again. Above the salutation was a Bible verse, Mark 11:24. It read, *Therefore I tell you, whatever you ask for in prayer, believe that you have received it, and it will be yours.*

Lacey took a deep breath and began reading the letter.

My Dearest Lacey Lou,

Today is your first birthday. Your mother and I are having a party for you this evening. Your mother has baked you a special cake, and Grandpa and Grandma will be celebrating with us.

We are so thankful to God for you. You are a special blessing. We miss Luke every day, but the joy that you have brought us has been so abundant. Although today is special because of you, it's also special because you are officially ours. The adoption is final.

I only wish I had put off my doctor's appointment for a little longer. My doctor told me I may not have as much time left as he initially thought. I need more time with your mother and my baby girl. I worry about not being here for both of you.

Lacey Lou, if there's one thing I long to teach you, it's that you can go to God and ask Him for anything you need. He will hear you, and He promises to help you. Read Mark 11:24 over and over and believe it.

I admit that I don't have all the answers to life's problems. I don't know why we lost Luke, and I don't know why I'm sick. I just know that God is in control. Even when we can't see the road, God knows the path. Remember that.

Please know how much I love you,
Daddy

Lacey set the letter down on the open Bible. Tears ran down her cheeks at the sweetness of his words. She wiped her face with her hands as she let his words sink in. She stared at the Christmas tree. Her thoughts were tumbling. *My father was sick? But didn't he die in a car accident? I was adopted? Hannah must have been my biological mother. She must have died at the delivery.*

Feelings of both sadness and anger surfaced as she tried to digest what she had learned. Why hadn't her mother told her any of this? Why would she keep something so important from her? Lacey couldn't understand her mother's secrecy. She needed to know more.

Lacey folded the letter and set it aside. She thumbed carefully through the rest of the Bible, but there weren't any more letters. Out of frustration and exhaustion, her eyes filled with tears. She felt sad and lost.

Why would my birth mother give me away? Why did my father get sick? What happened to Hannah and Luke? Is my biological father alive? If he is, does he even know about me? Why didn't they want Luke and me? Why didn't mom tell me?

As hard as Lacey tried to suppress them, she felt feelings of betrayal by her mother. Her father's first letter had mentioned sheltering Lacey from pain. *Is that it? Is that why no one ever told me these things?* For the first time, Lacey understood why she had yearned to know her family and her heritage. Subconsciously, she had known there were missing pieces. Her heart had known there was more to her story.

Lacey started to hyperventilate. Her tears had turned to sobs. Too many stressful events had occurred. She still felt a heartache over George, she had moved across the country to take a new job, and she was living in her childhood home with too many unsolved mysteries and vague memories. Her job had also presented stressors that made her doubt herself. And now, she had learned that she was adopted, once had a brother, and that her father may have died from a sickness instead of an accident.

Lacey picked up the Bible and held it to her chest. She was overwhelmed. She prayed, *Father, help me. I'm struggling. This is all too much. I don't think I can handle any more. Give me strength and help me through this. Help me understand. Please send me some comfort.*

Lacey's prayer was interrupted by a knock at the door. She wiped her eyes with her hands and set the Bible down. She hadn't expected company, and this really wasn't a good time for a visitor. Perhaps Barbie had decided to check on her.

Lacey unlocked the front door and opened it. To her surprise, Geret stood looking back at her.

Chapter Twenty-Two

"Hi there," said Geret, wearing a smile. He appeared to be trying to read Lacey.

Lacey gave him a half-smile. She knew her eyes were red, and her face was swollen from crying. "Come in out of the cold," she said.

Geret stepped inside and closed the door. "Is this a bad time? I can come back," he said.

"No. I mean, yes, but it's fine that you're here. Please come in," she replied, as she walked into the living room.

Geret removed his boots and followed her into the living room. He said, "You look upset. You've been crying."

Lacey turned to look at him and replied, "It's been a really hard morning, and I didn't sleep well."

"Understandable," he said.

"It's more than that," she said.

Geret furrowed his eyebrows, looking concerned. "What else is going on?"

Lacey exhaled and sat down on the couch. Then she looked at him, raising one eyebrow. "Aren't you supposed to be working today?"

Geret removed his coat and sat down beside her. He said, "I am, but I got someone to cover me for a bit. I called you at your office, but Barbie said you canceled your office to stay home today. I wanted to check on you."

Lacey nodded and said, "That was really nice. Thank you. Do you want some coffee?"

"Coffee sounds great," he replied.

"C'mon," she said.

Geret followed her to the kitchen. She poured him a cup of coffee and then filled her mug again. They sat down at the kitchen table. They were both quiet. Lacey liked Geret's unhurried, gentle nature. She liked that he wasn't pushy or demanding. He seemed content to just sit with her.

"So, tell me, how are you?" He asked after several minutes of just sitting with her.

"As you probably know, I've been better," she replied.

"You were so upset last night, which is understandable. You really had me concerned," he said.

"Were you convinced I was going to jump off a mountain?" She asked with the hint of a playful tone to her voice.

"Nothing like that. I just know how scared you were. It was a scary situation for everyone, even for me; and I came in on the tail end of it. I just worried about you being alone. I knew you would need to talk this out with someone," he said.

"Thanks. To be honest with you, I'm more upset about something else this morning," she said. Then she added, "I mean, I talked to Dr. Dean today, and the patient and baby are doing well. I realize there was a problem with the pre-packed surgery kit. It was missing a blade handle. That can be remedied."

"It has already been remedied, and I assure you it will never happen again," he said with resolution in his voice.

"Geret, I know you will see to it that the kits are perfect. It wasn't your fault. I'm not blaming anyone. I hope you know that. It was just a bad situation," she said.

"I know. I'm just looking at it from a quality perspective. We can't afford mistakes like that," he said.

Lacey nodded in agreement.

"So, what else is on your mind?" he asked.

She looked up at him and exhaled. Then she said, "Let's go sit by the fire. It's cold in here."

Lacey and Geret filled their coffee cups, and then Geret followed Lacey to the couch. They sat down on opposite ends, facing each other.

Lacey asked, "Remember when you asked me about my father's Bible?"

Geret nodded.

"Well, I found a letter in it that my father wrote to me on the day I was born. Wait, let me show you," she said. Lacey reached for the Bible and pulled the note out of Proverbs. She handed it to Geret.

Geret took the note, unfolded it, and read it. Afterward, he looked up at her and asked, "You had a twin brother?"

Lacey closed her eyes for a moment and exhaled. She said, "That was my first thought too. Then I was upset that my mother never told me about him. I couldn't understand why she wouldn't tell me. I figured there had to be more to the story."

"Is there more?" He asked.

"Well, this morning, I woke up feeling distraught from the overnight events. I opened my father's Bible for comfort. I was thumbing through it when I found a second letter ... in the book of Mark. My father wrote it to me on my first birthday."

"What did it say?" He asked.

Lacey reached for the second letter and opened it. She handed it to him.

Geret read the letter. After reading it, he handed it back to her. He had a look of surprise on his face. "So, I take it from this letter that you're adopted, and that your biological mother died during your birth, along with Luke."

Lacey nodded and said, "That's what I took away from it. I also learned that my father was sick. I don't think he was killed in an accident. I think he died from an illness."

Geret shook his head, and said, "That's a lot of heavy information to take on after the night you had. I'm sorry. What can I do?"

Lacey half-smiled at him and said, "I just appreciate your interest. It's good to be able to tell someone. I feel angry with my mom now. Why didn't she tell me I was adopted? Why wouldn't she tell me the truth about my dad? It's honestly hurtful. I feel sort of betrayed."

Geret scooted toward her on the couch. He took her hand in his and leaned in toward her. He said, "Look, I know your first reaction is to be angry with your mother. You don't know her reasons. You know how much she loved you. Try to give her the benefit of the doubt until you know more. You've had a lot of stuff dumped on you at once. Give yourself some time to process all of this. There have to be more answers."

Lacey wiped a tear from her cheek and sniffled. She replied, "I know you're right. I'm just emotional right now."

Geret said, "It's completely understandable."

Geret was interrupted when his cell phone rang. "Excuse me a minute. I have to answer this." After he disconnected the call, he said, "I need to get back to work."

Lacey nodded and stood to walk him to the door.

Geret put his coat and boots on and then stood by the door looking at her.

Lacey said, "Well, be safe, and have a good day."

Geret stepped toward her and took her in his arms. Lacey melted into his embrace and felt a surge of comfort from his touch.

"I thought you could use a hug. I needed one, too," he said.

"Thank you," she said.

He stepped back and asked playfully, "So, I'll see you on Friday for Christmas dinner?"

She nodded, "Yes, right."

As he opened the door to walk out, he turned to her one more time. With a more serious tone, he said, "I'll be praying for you."

Lacey closed the door and sat on the couch. *Jen and Katy won't believe what's been going on in my life.* She picked up her cell phone and sent a group text to both ladies. She sent a long text about the letters and how she had found them. Then she told them about her scary surgical case.

Both ladies replied adding their surprise and asking more questions.

After several texts, Lacey decided to lighten up the mood and wrote, "I wanted to tell you both that I think I met someone."

Immediately Katy texted back, "Oh my! Spill the beans … all of them!"

Jen wrote, "Ditto! I'm so excited! Who is he? Tell us everything!"

Lacey proceeded to tell them about Geret, how they met, and all of their interactions so far. Then she told them how they were having their first dinner on Christmas Day.

Katy texted, "So give me a description of this man. Tall, dark, and handsome?"

Jen texted, "Or insanely gorgeous and irresistible?"

Lacey smiled wide and shook her head. She loved these women and their spunky personalities. Oh, how she missed them. She wrote back, "He's incredibly handsome, built like a rock, and has a heart of gold."

Katy replied, "Sounds dreamy. You deserve a man like that."

Jen added, "Totally. So happy for you. Keep us posted or we'll hunt you down!"

Lacey sent back a thumbs up emoji and said, "I will. I miss you both. Love you both. Merry Christmas!"

Chapter Twenty-Three

On Friday morning, Lacey woke up around five o'clock. She glanced toward the window, and it was still dark outside. Her body felt heavy as she tried to roll to her side. With her first attempt to move, her body screamed in pain. She felt overwhelmed with body aches and soreness.

The night before at the hospital, Lacey started to feel bad. Her throat had been sore, her face had felt flushed, and she had started having cold chills. She had asked Veronica to check her temperature.

"Dr. Bartlett! You're sick!" Veronica had exclaimed when the thermometer registered 103.5.

Lacey went to bed at eight o'clock the night before, thinking that she just needed some extra rest. This morning, as she moved to get out of bed, she felt pain throughout her body. Even the friction from the sheets made her skin hurt. Her body was freezing with chills, yet her skin felt like it was on fire, and she knew her temperature was high, again. She proceeded with great effort to sit up and walk to the bathroom. Her head and neck felt heavy and sore. Her sinuses were congested, and her throat burned. She struggled back toward her bed. Every step hurt, and she barely had enough energy to get back to her bed.

She thought of Geret and their planned Christmas dinner for today. There was no way she would be good company. She picked up the phone and texted, "Good morning. Sorry to text so early. I have a fever and body aches. Not sure, but it might be the flu. Sorry, but I have to cancel our dinner today. We can do it again soon. Merry Christmas."

Geret answered, "I'm sorry. What can I do for you?"

Lacey texted back, "Nothing. I'm going back to bed."

Geret texted, "Okay. Please feel better. Text or call me if you need anything. Merry Christmas."

Lacey took some Tylenol and then crawled back into bed. She didn't wake up again until five o'clock that evening. Her temperature was down to 101, but her body aches were almost unbearable. In addition, she had started to cough. Lacey forced herself to drink some hot tea and eat some soup. Her appetite was down, but she was thankful that she had no nausea. After being awake for only an hour, she couldn't remember ever feeling this exhausted. She took more Tylenol and then crawled back into bed and slept.

Lacey stayed in bed all weekend and only got up for water, Tylenol, soup, and to go to the bathroom. By Monday, she wasn't feeling any better. She called Barbie on Monday morning and asked her to reschedule her patients for later in the week. Barbie expressed her concern and told Lacey she was coming by to see her. Lacey objected because she didn't want Barbie to get her illness, but Barbie promised to stop by for only a few minutes. She wanted to bring Lacey some soup and hot tea. Since Barbie had insisted on coming over, Lacey took a short, hot shower. She had hoped to feel better after the shower, but instead, she felt lightheaded and had to lie down.

When the doorbell rang, Lacey slowly moved toward it and let Barbie in. "Oh, Dr. B, ya look awful, honey," Barbie said with a worried tone in her voice.

"I'll be okay. I just need rest," Lacey said.

"Okay, well, I brought ya some chicken noodle soup and hot tea. Is it the flu?" Barbie asked.

"Probably," Lacey replied.

"Dr. B, you've been working too much. You're worn down. That's why you're sick," Barbie said.

"You're probably right. Thanks for bringing this soup and tea for me. You need to get out of here before I make you sick," Lacey said as she started to scold Barbie.

"I think ya need to see a doctor," Barbie said, sounding motherly.

"I am a doctor. I'll be fine," Lacey said, feeling tired and growing impatient.

"Okay, well promise me you'll call me if ya need anything," Barbie pleaded.

"I will. Thanks, Barbie. Be careful," Lacey said softly, as she nudged Barbie out the door and closed and locked it behind her.

The next day, Lacey got up only twice to drink tea and eat soup. Despite the Tylenol, she continued to feel weak, and her cough grew worse. She was still having intermittent fevers, but now, she felt weaker. As she lay in bed that evening, she felt utterly alone. She had been sick at home for five days, and she had been visited by one person, her only friend in Pocatello. She pondered her situation. *What if I die here alone? How long would it take for someone to find me?* At that thought and because of her misery, Lacey started to cry. Then she started to pray and fell asleep.

The sound of the doorbell woke Lacey. Her room was dark, and she wasn't sure what day or time it was. She heard the doorbell a second time and assumed that Barbie had come to check on her again. She slowly made her way to the door. As the door swung open, Lacey was surprised to see Geret standing in front of her. She knew she looked awful, but she was too weak to feel mortified. Despite her embarrassment and desire to be hidden from view, she felt a hint of relief to have human contact. She opened the door wider to let him in.

The look on Geret's face was troubled. "Lacey, are you okay? You look really sick." Lacey felt dizzy and must have started to sway because Geret reached out and took hold of her arms. He closed the door and guided Lacey back to her bed. "Here, lie down," he said.

Lacey lay down and looked up at him. "What are you doing here?" She asked weakly.

Geret replied, "I texted you a few times, and you didn't reply. So, I got a little worried, and I called Barbie. She told me how sick you were and that you had canceled your office until later this week. That made me worry a bit more. I had to come check on you."

Lacey looked at him. "Thank you, but you should go. I'll make you sick."

Geret looked concerned, and said, "I think you might have the flu."

Lacey weakly replied, "Yes, I'm pretty sure I do, even though I got a flu shot this year."

Geret leaned closer to her and touched her forehead while she lay on the bed. He asked, "Has anyone been here to take care of you?" He seemed to know the answer before she answered.

"Just Barbie, once. I wouldn't let her come back," Lacey said as she started to tear up.

Geret stared at her with an empathetic look, before he propped Lacey up on two pillows.

"Hold on," Geret said as he disappeared into the kitchen. She could hear him shuffling through drawers and cabinets.

He returned a few minutes later with a thermometer and a cup of hot tea. "Open your mouth," Geret directed. Lacey complied as Geret stuck a thermometer under her tongue. "No fever right now. Drink this slowly," he said.

She took a few sips and then fell asleep.

Several hours later, Geret nudged Lacey's arm to wake her. He startled her, and she opened her eyes and looked at him. She vaguely remembered how he had come to the door and put her back in bed, and she wondered if she had been dreaming.

"You need to eat something," Geret said softly. "Here," he said as he fed her a few spoonfuls of warm, chicken noodle soup.

Opening her mouth, she didn't say a word, but was able to eat a few bites and then take the Tylenol he gave her. She then lay back on the pillow and fell back to sleep.

Chapter Twenty-Four

Geret brewed a pot of coffee in Lacey's kitchen. After he poured a cup, he sat down at the table. Glancing out the window, he noticed it was dark, but he could see the snow falling under the glow of the outdoor lights. He looked at his watch, and it was almost midnight. Lacey coughed, and he turned his head toward her room to make sure she wasn't calling for him. The last thing he would do at this point was leave her.

He glanced at the wall beside the table and noticed a painted picture of a bouquet of flowers that appeared to be a bridal bouquet. There were several different bold and colorful flowers in it. Geret wasn't sure what they all were, but there were yellow daisies, red roses, and some kind of white and blue flowers. There were sprigs of greenery and baby's breath scattered throughout the bouquet. Geret was struck by the simplicity and beauty of it. Though the flowers were so different from each other, together they were beautiful. He looked closer and saw that there were words underneath the painting. The words were *Covenant Bouquet.*

Geret heard Lacey cough again. He started to scold himself for not coming to see her sooner. His pride had kept him away. When Lacey canceled Friday morning by text message, he figured she had changed her mind. He knew there were rumors about him in Pocatello, and he feared that she had heard them.

When Darla had tried to come back to him after Reese dumped her, he had refused to take her back. He knew that if she could cheat once, she would do it again. She had broken his heart and his trust. When Darla couldn't convince him to take her back, she started a rumor that he had cheated on her first.

It took some time for the rumor to fade away. Although Geret was over Darla, he still felt bad for her. She wasn't a bad person. She had, unfortunately, allowed herself to become wrapped up with fame and the paparazzi. The tabloids had exploded with embellished stories of Reese's break-up with her.

He thought Lacey had heard the rumors and changed her mind about him. She already seemed guarded, and he wondered who had broken her heart. There were rumors that she moved to Pocatello to leave behind an ex-boyfriend. No one knew the details, though, and Geret didn't feel right asking about it.

Lacey had another coughing attack. Then Geret heard a wretching noise. He quickly walked into her room. She was sitting up at the bedside. She looked up with glassy eyes when she saw the light from the hallway.

Lacey started to cry and was swaying to keep her balance. She cried, "I threw up."

Geret could see how miserable she felt. He walked over to her and said, "It's okay. Let me help you."

Lacey said, "No, this is disgusting." Then she furrowed her eyebrows and looked up at him, and asked, "Why are you still here?"

Geret replied, "I'm staying here to take care of you. You need me."

Lacey felt weak and started to fall backward onto the bed. Geret caught her back and held her up. He said, "C'mon, let me get you cleaned up."

Geret helped her stand and walked her into the bathroom. He sat her on the closed toilet. He helped her gently lift her pajama top off. She was wearing a black camisole underneath. It was still clean. Her pajama bottoms were still clean and dry, too. Geret soaked a washcloth in hot water and then squeezed out the excess water from it. He knelt down on one knee beside her and cleaned off her face and neck.

Lacey felt dizzy. She reached up and set her left hand on Geret's shoulder to keep her balance. "I'm dizzy," she said.

Geret couldn't help but notice the scar under her left arm. It was quite extensive, and he couldn't help but wonder what it was from. Without thinking, he ran his fingers over the scar trying to understand its source.

Lacey reflexively jerked her arm down and pulled away.

"Sorry," Geret said. "I just saw the scar, and the nurse in me was curious what it was from."

Lacey exhaled, looking down at the floor. To her surprise, she was alarmed at Geret seeing the scar.

"You don't have to tell me, it's okay. We can forget about it," he said.

"I had breast cancer when I was thirty. I had to have radiation and a mastectomy on that side," she said.

Geret stared at her in shock. Then with empathy in his eyes, he asked, "Are you okay now?"

Lacey nodded her head.

Geret finished cleaning off Lacey's face with the warm washcloth. Lacey couldn't look up at him. She felt nervous after telling him about her scars. He now knew she had a reconstructed breast. She didn't know why, but it bothered her that he knew. She wondered what he would think of her, knowing this. She hoped he wouldn't find her scars offensive.

Geret dried Lacey's face off gently with a dry towel. As he did, he could sense her self-consciousness. Her history with breast cancer had obviously scarred her not only physically, but also emotionally. He reached for her chin and tilted her face up to his and said, "I personally think you are beautiful."

Lacey just stared at him in disbelief. Her heart felt enveloped in warmth, and she suddenly found herself wanting to be engulfed in his arms. She leaned forward into him, and he held her. She whispered, "Thank you."

After a moment, Geret said, "Let's get you back to bed." Geret took her to the couch and laid her down with a pillow and blanket. He flipped on the fireplace switch.

He said, "I'm going to change your sheets, and then I'll help you back to bed."

Lacey opened her eyes for a moment and said, "Thank you so much." Then she closed her eyes and fell back to sleep.

Geret looked in the hallway closet, then in Lacey's closet, and then in the laundry room. He was in search of clean sheets, but he couldn't find any. After putting the soiled sheets and Lacey's pajama top in the washer, he added some detergent and then started the wash cycle. He went back into her bedroom and noticed the wardrobe. *Maybe there are sheets in there.* He walked over and opened the wardrobe doors and saw that it was empty. As he went to close the doors, a picture frame caught his eye. It was lying in the bottom right corner.

He picked it up and looked at it. It was a framed photograph of Lacey in a beautiful, yellow gown with a handsome stranger in a black tux. They both looked happy. *She looks beautiful,* he thought. Geret grimaced at the sight of the man in the picture. *This must be the guy,* he reasoned. Geret replaced the picture and closed the wardrobe. He decided he would stop looking for extra sheets and just wait on the laundry. He didn't want to go through Lacey's things, nor did he want to find any more happy pictures of her with another guy.

When the laundry was done, Geret made Lacey's bed. He took a thermometer, a glass of water with Tylenol, and Lacey's pajama top to the living room where Lacey was sleeping. Lacey stirred when she heard Geret.

"Hey," Lacey said. She felt a little better. Her body aches seemed less, and her soreness was gone.

"Hi there," replied Geret. "How are you feeling?"

"A little better," Lacey replied.

"I'm glad you're awake. I made your bed, and I have your clean pajama top for you," said Geret.

Lacey sat up, took the pajama top from Geret, and put it on. "Thank you," she said.

"Let me take your temperature," he said.

"I think my fever is gone," Lacey said, as she opened her mouth for the thermometer.

Geret said, "98.6. Much better." He handed her two Tylenol tablets and said, "Go ahead and take these."

Lacey complied by swallowing the pills with a gulp of water. Then she drank the rest of the water in the cup. "I was thirsty," she said.

"You look better," he said. "Are you hungry?"

"No, I'm feeling tired again," she replied.

"Let me help you back to your bed," he said.

Lacey nodded and then leaned forward as he helped her walk to her bed. Within seconds, she was asleep again.

Geret felt exhausted. He wandered back into the living room and lay on the couch. He set his watch alarm for six o'clock. It was now two in the morning. He knew his workday was going to be a tough one with his lack of sleep.

It didn't bother him, though. He knew there wasn't anywhere else he'd rather be right now.

Chapter Twenty-Five

Later that morning, Lacey woke up with a feeling she hadn't felt for some time—energy. The aches had gone away, and she felt like getting out of bed. As she sat up, she suddenly had the recollection that Geret had visited her the day before. She then remembered how he had fed her soup and tea and cleaned her up when she threw up. *Was it all a dream?*

She slowly rose and opened her bedroom door to peek out. No one was there. She pulled her robe and slippers on and meandered to the kitchen. It was quiet. It seemed like an eternity since she'd been out in her kitchen, though it had only been about five days. The kitchen was clean. The dishes in the sink had been washed and put away. Lacey glanced at the coffee maker and saw a piece of paper taped to it. She walked over and lifted the paper to read it. *"Lacey, I hope you are feeling better. If you need anything, please call or text me. Btw, there is more soup in your pantry, Take care, Geret."*

She smiled softly shaking her head. "I guess it wasn't a dream," she said under her breath. Geret had been there. She tried to remember everything that had happened, but the details were fuzzy. She didn't understand why he would stay to care for her, but she felt a deep sense of gratitude.

As she thought about it more, she surmised that, had the roles been reversed, she probably would have done the same thing. After all, caring for sick people is what both Geret and

Lacey did for a living. She didn't want to make a big deal out of it. Still, she was touched by this simple act of kindness and compassion. She wondered if he was dating anyone. She was sure a man that looked as good as he did would have a girlfriend. *What if he has a girlfriend, like George, but felt obligated to help me since I have no one? Could he actually care for me?*

Self-doubt entered her mind. *No, he is just a good-hearted guy. He knows I really don't have anyone.* She decided to shake off her thoughts. She picked up her cell phone and checked her messages. There were none. She sighed out loud at that. Then she called Barbie at the office.

"Dr. Bartlett, are ya feeling better? You sound better."

"Yes, I feel much better. Thanks for checking on me this week." Lacey replied.

"Can I do anything for ya?" Barbie asked.

Lacey said, "Yes, I was calling to ask you to open up my schedule for tomorrow. I'm sure I have a lot to catch up on."

"Sure thing," Barbie replied with her usual bouncing energy. Then she added, "I have a lot of messages and labs for you to review. I sorted everything into piles on your desk."

Lacey cringed at the thought of the work awaiting her. "Okay, thanks. You're the best."

Lacey decided not to say anything about Geret since she didn't want to make more out of his concern for her than was really there. She brewed some coffee and thought about how much she had missed the aroma and taste. The first sip was delicious. She closed her eyes and exhaled, "Mmm."

In the living room, she flipped on the fireplace switch and lowered herself down onto the couch. Her movements were still very slow. She pulled the blanket over her legs, and then her cell phone chirped. There was a text from Geret, and she felt her stomach flip-flop.

"Just wanted to check on you. I hope you are feeling better. Please let me know if you need anything."

Lacey just stared at the message for a minute and then typed, "I'm feeling much better, and I'm going back to work tomorrow. How can I ever repay you?"

"Not necessary. I wanted to help."

She wrote back, "I owe you dinner," followed by a smiley face. He sent a smiley face back. She stared at the phone in her hands for a while. For the first time in a long time, Lacey's downtrodden heart felt a little lighter, and she smiled.

Lacey ate some oatmeal, then showered and threw on some leggings and an oversized sweatshirt. She decided to clean her germ-infested house now that she was feeling better. She washed her bedsheets, cleaned her bathroom, and vacuumed the floors. When she was satisfied with the cleanliness of her home, she showered and then collapsed on the couch. After a few moments of rest, she got up to turn on the fireplace and to start one of her feel-good movies. Exhausted from taking on a little too much in her recovering state, she collapsed back onto the couch and pulled a blanket over herself. Within minutes, she was asleep.

When she woke up, it was dark outside. The time on the wall clock was 7:15. She wasn't sure if it was morning or night, and she panicked that she might be late for work. Reaching for her cell phone, she saw it was 7:15 p.m., and she breathed a sigh of relief. As she stood up from the couch, her stomach growled. She hadn't eaten lunch or dinner. She went into the kitchen pantry and pulled out a can of soup.

The doorbell rang. Lacey looked up toward the door, unable to imagine who it might be. *Maybe Barbie is stopping by, or maybe Geret is checking on me?* She felt a sense of excited anticipation when she thought it might be Geret. She glanced at herself in the mirror and tried to calm down her bed head.

She walked to the door and could feel her heart pounding in her chest. She opened the door, and the spark of excitement she felt disappeared as quickly as it had ignited. Standing there, leaning casually against the doorway with crossed arms and a big smile, was Rusty Simms.

Lacey tried not to frown but was sure her look was one of indifference. Although she tried to be friendly, she just felt annoyed.

"Hey," she said as she motioned for him to step in out of the cold so she could close the door.

Rusty looked her over, "Hey there, did you just wake up?"

She answered him wearily, "Yes."

Rusty ignored her disdain and said, "Well, I've been meaning to connect with you. So, when you weren't at work today, I thought it might be the perfect opportunity for me to stop by." Then he added, "This is a pretty old place. I'm surprised you haven't bought one of those new condos in town. Plus, it doesn't make sense for you to live out in the boondocks."

She looked away, rolling her eyes, and answered, "I love this house. It's been in my family for years. Besides, I like being in the boondocks. It doesn't encourage people to just stop by."

Rusty looked at her snidely. "Well, so when are you free? I'll show you around. We can grab some dinner."

Lacey didn't appreciate his arrogance or his intrusion. She was growing more irritated with every moment of his presence, and she found it odd that he had just stopped by. She replied, "I really don't know. I'm still recovering from the flu, and I don't really have the energy for company. I wish you would have called first because I think I might still be contagious."

Rusty suddenly looked alarmed. He said, "The flu? You know, you don't actually look that good. I really can't be sick, so I should probably come back when you're better. I'll get going. Call me when you're feeling better, and we'll get together," he said.

Rusty replaced his gloves and walked toward the door.

Lacey followed him and opened the door. "Thanks for stopping by," she said.

He turned to say something to her, but Lacey didn't wait for a response from him. She closed the door and locked it. *What an annoying, self-centered man*, she thought.

A few minutes later, there was a knock at the door. Lacey exhaled. *Can he seriously not take a hint? What does he want now?* Lacey's irritation with Rusty had reached a maximum threshold. *What a pain!* She looked around the room to see if maybe he had forgotten something. Annoyed and perturbed, she walked briskly to the door. She unlocked the deadbolt and flung the door open with force and frustration.

Geret stared at her with wide eyes as he stood in the doorway. Her face suddenly flushed, and she felt her stomach leap into her throat as she stared up at him.

"I'm sorry, were you expecting someone else? Maybe, someone you wanted to hit over the head with a bat?" Geret asked when he saw the irritated look on her face. "If this is a bad time ..." he added.

"No, no," Lacey stammered, "It's a great time. Please come in. I'm sorry. I just had an unwanted visitor I finally got rid of, and I thought you were ..." she trailed off looking at Geret.

"Him?" He asked as she motioned him inside. He then added, "I saw Rusty Simms leaving your driveway when I drove down your street."

"Yes," she replied. "He was not invited, and I couldn't get him to leave."

Geret looked at her, feeling a little uneasy. "Oh, well, I know I wasn't invited, but I just wanted to check on you. I brought you dinner. I hope you don't mind, and I won't stay."

Lacey smiled at him and exhaled. "I'm very happy to see you, Geret. Please come in and stay for a while."

Lacey walked toward the couch, and Geret followed her. "Did I interrupt an argument or something?" Geret asked.

Lacey replied, "No. He just showed up here out of the blue. So strange."

Geret raised an eyebrow and said, "I think he has an agenda."

Lacey whirled around to face Geret, stopping him in his tracks. She said, "Well, if his agenda is me, he's not going to get far. I have zero interest in someone like him."

"Someone like him?" Geret asked.

Lacey cocked her head to one side and asked, "Do I really have to spell it out?"

"Okay," Geret said with his hands up in the air in a surrender position.

Lacey chuckled and said, "Sorry. He is one of the cockiest, most selfish men I've ever met. He asked me out, and instead of answering him, I reminded him that I might still be contagious. He couldn't leave fast enough because he didn't want to get sick. He's one of those guys who really only cares about number one." She let out a big sigh and asked, "Can I get you something?"

Geret handed her the bag he was holding. "No, I'm fine. Thanks. This is pasta from Giuseppi's. I hope you like pasta."

Lacey replied, "Yes, thank you. I'm starving, and I was about to fix myself something to eat. Would you like to join me?"

Geret smiled at her, "Sure. Why not? I actually left my food in my truck because I figured you didn't want company. I was going to eat it when I got home. I'll go get it."

Lacey gave him a warm smile. "Would you like a glass of wine?"

Geret smiled back at her, "Sure." When Geret returned from outside, Lacey had disappeared into her bathroom to freshen up.

She heard him come back in and yelled, "Your wine is on the table in the kitchen. I'll be right there."

Lacey looked at herself in the mirror. She was horrified. "Oh my gosh. I look awful," she whispered. She brushed her hair and threw it into a ponytail. Then she applied a little makeup. She removed her oversized sweatshirt and slipped into a more fitting sweater. Finally, she added one squirt of perfume. *There, that's better.* She shouldn't care how she looked right now, but she did.

When Lacey returned to the kitchen, Geret was seated at the table sipping his wine. He said, "This tastes great. Thank you."

Lacey replied, "I'm glad you like it. I'm going to pass on a glass myself. I need to hydrate."

Geret smiled. "I completely agree." Geret had not yet removed his dinner from the carryout bag.

"You didn't have to wait for me," Lacey said, surprised.

"I wanted to eat with you," Geret said softly, looking directly at her.

Lacey sat down at the table across from Geret. Geret pulled both meals out of the bags and set them on the table. "Hold on," Lacey said, as she stood. She walked over to a drawer and pulled out silverware. She returned to the table and sat down while handing Geret a fork and knife. "Food tastes better when your fork isn't plastic."

Geret smiled and said, "Thanks. That is so true. That's all I eat with at the hospital. It's nice to use the real stuff sometimes."

While they ate, they talked about the hospital, the operating room, and some of the people they worked with. Although they talked easily about various subjects, neither of them discussed their past relationships.

Lacey was surprised at how comfortable and relaxed she felt with Geret. Not once did the conversation feel forced or awkward. She found herself wanting to know more about him, and she enjoyed hearing him talk. He was so easy to look at as well. She stared at his sculpted jawline, and his big, broad shoulders. *He is really gorgeous.*

Lacey had finished eating and had perched her elbows on the table. She leaned her chin onto her hands and was looking at Geret.

"Lacey?" Geret asked with an inquiring look.

When he said her name, her thoughts came back to reality. She flinched, and her face flushed as she realized her train of thought had not been on his words. Trying to divert his attention away from her face, she quickly got up from the table to take their plates to the sink. She said, "Here, let me take these."

Geret stood and said, "Let me take care of the cleanup."

Lacey shook her head and said, "No, you've already done so much for me. I can't thank you enough. I need to do something for you."

After Lacey threw the trash away, she turned to face Geret. She didn't realize he had followed her and was standing right in front of her now.

Geret's movement was slow and with purpose. He reached for both of her hands and held them gently in his. He said, "I came to take care of you because I wanted to. You were sick, and I didn't want you to be alone. You don't owe me anything. I did it because I care for you."

Lacey just stood there looking at him. She couldn't believe how easily he had spoken the words. He didn't trip over them. He didn't stutter through them. He didn't make any excuses. He told her straight up how he felt. She wasn't used to this. It had taken George over five years to admit he had feelings for her, and when she asked for more, he just didn't know.

"Thank you," she finally said.

Geret smiled at her, squeezed her hands gently and let go. Then he said, "I need to get going. You need to go to bed. It's almost ten o'clock. You need rest."

Lacey felt disappointment rush through her. She didn't want him to go. She liked having him close. She wanted to hear more about how he cared for her. But she relented and replied, "Okay, sure. You're right. I have a full day of office patients tomorrow."

Geret turned to walk out of the kitchen, and he stopped and pointed to the picture on the wall he had noticed the night before. He asked, "What is a *covenant bouquet*?"

Lacey smiled. She said, "That is a painting of my grandmother's wedding bouquet. My grandfather made it for her." She reached up and removed the painting from the wall and turned it over. There was an inscription on the back. Lacey read it out loud to Geret. "'Dear Vivie, I pledge to protect you, love you always, and to never leave you. I have made you this covenant bouquet as a reminder of our wedding day and my promises to you. Forever yours, Joe, April 14, 1950.'" Lacey replaced the painting on the wall.

Geret said, "That's an amazing kind of love."

Lacey said, "They are such a good example of committed love." She paused and then added, "This is the only painting I have that was theirs."

Geret said, "It's definitely one to treasure." He lifted his coat from the kitchen chair and put it on while he walked to the door. He turned the doorknob and then looked at her with an endearing smile. "Get some rest and when you get tired tomorrow, don't push yourself. I'm glad you're feeling better. Thanks for having dinner with me."

The softness in his voice was genuine. It caught Lacey off guard. She wasn't used to this kind of sincerity from a man. When he looked at her, he made her feel like she was the only person in the world who mattered. He made her feel special.

"Thanks for checking on me," she said.

Geret started to turn the doorknob to open the door when he stopped and turned to face Lacey again. He started to say something but then stopped, as if he were trying to decide if he wanted to say what he was going to say. Finally, he said, "Look, I don't want to come across the wrong way."

Lacey's heart sank at these words. He was going to tell her he just wanted to be friends with her. She waited for him to say more.

Geret continued, "But, I really like you. I know it may not be wise to date someone you work with, but would you have dinner with me this Friday night?"

Lacey's heart and face lit up upon hearing his words. She smiled at him and replied, "I would love to."

Geret nodded and smiled. Then he whispered, "Sleep well. Good night."

"Good night," Lacey replied.

With that, he opened the door and disappeared into the night.

Lacey leaned against the closed door. She had an uneasy, yet excited, feeling. *I like him*, she thought and smiled. This man made her heart skip a beat and her knees weak. She felt herself drawn to him physically and emotionally. This man had taken care of her when she was sick; and from her short time spent with him, he seemed authentic. *Plus, he likes me.*

Lacey exhaled loudly, and her smile faded. Self-doubt started to flood her thoughts. She needed a reality check. She really didn't know Geret. Their time together had been limited, and trusting a man with her heart would not come easily for her. Lacey grimaced as she thought. Then she prayed, "Lord, please show me if I can trust this man with my heart. Fill me with wisdom so that I don't keep making the same mistakes over and over."

Chapter Twenty-Six

2018

Lacey's Thursday night call that week was busy. By Friday morning at the end of call, she was exhausted. She had scheduled patients that morning in the office, so she didn't get home until two o'clock that afternoon. She went directly to sleep out of necessity. At four-thirty, she heard her cell phone ring.

"Hello?" She answered, sounding groggy.

"Hey there," said Geret.

"Hey," Lacey said, forcing a reply.

"It sounds like I woke you up. Why don't you go back to sleep and call me when you wake up again?" Geret asked.

"No, Geret, it's okay. I was going to call you in a few minutes. I had my alarm set for five."

"Okay, great. What time do you want me to pick you up?" He asked with excitement in his voice.

Lacey struggled to speak clearly, as she was still only half-awake. "Geret, I don't think I can go out tonight. I'm exhausted from my call last night. Please don't think I don't want to have dinner with you, because I really do."

Geret tried not to sound upset, and for a moment considered that Lacey had changed her mind. "Oh okay, if anyone understands how tired you are, I do. Just call me if you want to try for another night for dinner."

Lacey stopped Geret before he could hang up, "Wait, how about tomorrow night?"

Geret felt relieved and smiled to himself and said, "Sure. Pick you up at six?"

Lacey replied, "I will be ready. Thank you for understanding."

Geret said, "Get some rest, and I'll see you tomorrow."

The following evening, Lacey could feel butterflies fluttering around in her stomach. She wasn't sure why she felt nervous about dinner with Geret, but she did. She had been thinking about him all day in anticipation of seeing him at her doorstep. The flutters in her stomach had grown with each hour that passed.

Earlier that day on the phone, they had agreed to have dinner at Sonny's. It was the most contemporary restaurant in town, so Lacey decided to dress up. Despite the cold, January night, Lacey chose a long, black maxi-dress with long sleeves. She pulled her hair back and up loosely into a clip, allowing for the clipped hair to spill down over the clip. The loose hair curled softly. A few loose strands fell out of the clip and curled along her neck.

She slipped on the dress and then put on her long, black, suede boots. The dress had a side slit from the knee down. She added a pair of silver hoop earrings and a dainty silver chain with a small, diamond pendant. After applying makeup and a squirt of perfume, she looked at herself in the full-length mirror. It had been a while since she had dressed up. In fact, the last time she wore a more formal dress had been graduation. It felt good to feel pretty again. She smiled at herself in the mirror.

The doorbell rang at five minutes until six. Lacey opened the door to find a smiling Geret with wide eyes.

"Wow, you look gorgeous!" Geret exclaimed with a big smile.

"Thank you," Lacey replied. "You clean up pretty good yourself," she added. They both chuckled. Geret was wearing a dark gray shirt under a black jacket, black slacks, and black boots. He leaned in and gave Lacey a hug and kissed her cheek.

Lacey could feel her breath catch at his gentle show of affection. She caught a whiff of his aftershave and inhaled deeply. He smelled fresh, like soap and musk.

"You smell good," she said.

"Thanks, so do you," he replied. "Are you hungry?"

"I'm starving," she replied.

"Are you ready to go?" He asked.

Lacey nodded. She put on her coat and gloves and then locked the front door behind them. Geret helped her get into the passenger side of the truck, and then he climbed into the driver's side. He had kept the truck running with the heater on, so the cab felt toasty.

Because Sonny's was more of a big city restaurant, Lacey wondered how long it would be able to stay in business in Pocatello. When Geret and Lacey arrived, they were seated in a quiet corner at a table for two. Delicate drop lights hung over each individual table, giving off dim, romantic light. There was also a lighted candle as the centerpiece for each table. Soft music played over speakers in the background. Lacey felt like she was in the big city every time she stepped into Sonny's. She had been here a few times with Barbie for lunch and dinner.

The waiter brought the wine menu, and Geret and Lacey ordered red wine along with an appetizer.

"How do you like the wine?" Geret asked.

Lacey replied, "It's really good. It starts out smooth ... and I can taste cherry, mushroom, and a woodsy flavor. Then it has a bite at the end."

Geret smiled and said, "It sounds like you know your wine."

Lacey smiled, "Not really, but I've developed an appreciation for it in the last few years."

Geret cocked his head to one side and raised his eyebrow, "I don't know much about wine, but I definitely appreciate being with you tonight."

Lacey couldn't help but smile. She replied, "Thanks, I'm glad. Me, too."

They sat in awkward silence sipping on the wine, while they both glanced around the restaurant. Lacey could feel Geret's eyes on her, and she looked over at him.

"You are a very beautiful woman," he said.

Lacey could feel her cheeks flush, and she looked away. "Wow," she replied.

"What?" He asked sincerely.

She replied, "Either you are a very smooth talker or ..." She trailed off.

Geret finished her statement, "... or I'm a very honest man."

Her eyes met his gaze. He seemed to be looking right into her soul. She couldn't explain it, but just being with him gave her a sense of peace. He was comfortable, like home.

"What are you going to order?" She asked, trying to divert his attention elsewhere. He smiled and glanced at his menu.

He said, "I think I'll have steak tonight."

Lacey smiled at him, "That sounds good. I think I will, too."

They ordered dinner and enjoyed light conversation while they ate. Lacey was still tired from her Thursday night call, and Geret could see that. He wanted to ask her more about her past, but he refrained from taking their conversation too deep. She needed to be able to relax tonight, and he found himself just wanting to care for her. She had worked so hard and had given so much of herself to her patients. She was alone, too, and he understood loneliness.

When the waiter returned with the dessert menu, Geret and Lacey decided to split a slice of chocolate lava cake. After dessert, they sat in silence, sipping coffee. Geret leaned forward and reached his hand across the table. He took Lacey's hand in his and held it gently.

Lacey felt a surge of heat go through her body as his fingers wrapped around hers. She smiled at him, and then removed her hand gently, as she reached for her purse. "I owe you this dinner," she said.

"Why?" He asked.

"Because you took care of me when I was sick," she replied.

Geret shook his head. He said, "I told you before, you needed someone to take care of you, and I wanted to be there for you. I'm paying for dinner." He picked up the bill as the waiter set it on the table.

"Thank you for dinner. I can't remember the last time I had this much fun," Lacey said.

"It's been my pleasure," Geret replied.

Lacey chuckled and shook her head.

Geret looked at her, puzzled, and asked, "What are you laughing about?"

Lacey shook her head. She said, "Oh, nothing really. I was just thinking of the first day I sort of met you."

He furrowed his brows and asked, "What do you mean, sort of?"

She asked, "Do you remember the day you almost steamrolled me in front of the elevator?"

Geret tilted his head back and smiled wide. "That's not how I remember it. I was running down the hallway, to an emergency, and some pretty little thing just stepped out of the elevator right into my path without warning."

"Oh, is that how it happened?" She asked, teasing him.

Geret stood and walked over to her. His face turned a little more serious as he gently pulled her up from her seat. He pulled her to him and said, "I had to find an impressive way for you to notice me." Then he leaned down and pressed his lips to hers. He pulled back and looked at her. He asked, "Did it work?"

Lacey stood there, dumbfounded, and looked back at him. Her knees had become weak, and she thought they might buckle under her. Finally, she said, "Whatever you have done to get my attention has worked so far."

He smiled at her. "Are you ready to go?" He asked.

Lacey nodded and followed him out.

They headed back to Lacey's house. Neither of them wanted the evening to end. As they approached her house, she asked, "Would you like to come in for a while and have a glass of wine and play a game of pool?"

Geret looked at her and said, "Sure. That sounds great." Then he looked at her again, and asked, "You have a pool table?"

Lacey giggled, "Yeah, it's in the back room. I'll show you."

They headed into the kitchen, and Lacey set out two wine glasses on the table. Geret opened a bottle of Merlot and poured two glasses. Lacey kicked off her boots, and they headed back to the pool table.

"Are you a fan of Alabama?" Lacey asked as she fumbled through various CD's.

Geret grinned, "The Crimson Tide?"

Lacey looked at him with a smirk.

"Yes, I love Alabama's music," he said and chided, "Play me some mountain music ..."

Lacey laughed out loud. *He is so adorable.*

They played several games of pool and shared several laughs and stories. Lacey couldn't help but admire his arms and back, as he would stretch out with the pool stick just before hitting the cue ball.

Lacey caught Geret eyeing her several times when he thought she wasn't looking or hadn't noticed. A few times, as they walked past each other to maneuver around the pool table, they brushed up against each other. Geret brought her senses alive. She loved being near him and found herself feeling more relaxed as the evening wore on.

At midnight, Geret and Lacey settled in the living room on the couch. As they continued to talk, their playful banter turned to more personal conversation.

Lacey asked, "Why have you stayed in Pocatello? Someone told me you were from California and that you only came to Idaho to play football."

Geret could sense a feeling of uneasiness. He didn't want to talk about Darla, but he wanted to be sure Lacey knew the truth about his past. He replied, "I did come here to play football, and I had also planned to return to California after college." He paused, and then he said, "I'm not sure what you've heard about me, but I know there are some rumors circulating."

Lacey replied, "I asked Barbie about you. She told me what she had heard, but that's all."

Geret nodded. He said, "Well, as you probably know, I dated a girl named Darla. We were supposed to get married after college and live in LA. Long story short, she cheated with a Lakers' player. When he broke up with her, she tried to come back to me, and when I refused to reconcile with her, she tried to tell everyone that I cheated first. Eventually, she gave up on me. My life was a mess for a while when she came back here. So, I was so relieved when she left, and the truth came out. I don't harbor any ill feelings toward her, though. I actually feel sorry for her. She got caught up in being the girlfriend of someone famous. She always had a flair for wanting to be someone special."

"Someone special?" Lacey asked.

"Yeah, she just wanted to be famous. I thought that being a Lakers' dancer would be enough popularity for her, but apparently, it wasn't."

Lacey sat silently as she assimilated his story. She took a sip of wine and seemed lost in thought.

Geret asked, "Can I ask you a question?"

Lacey smiled. She answered, "Of course."

Geret said, "When you were sick, and I was looking for clean sheets to put on your bed, I found a framed photograph of you in a yellow dress with a guy in a tux. Was he ... or is he ... still important to you?"

Lacey exhaled and felt pain in her heart. Geret could see the change in her affect, and said, "You don't have to answer that."

She said, "No, it's okay. That guy is George Andreas. He was my plastic surgeon, by default. Several years after I was no longer his patient, we went out. The bottom line is that it didn't work out. He had been dating another woman off-and-on for several years. I think he was torn between the two of us for a short while, but he made his choice, and he married her."

Geret furrowed his eyebrows and asked, "What do you mean, 'by default?'"

Lacey replied, "I actually had a different plastic surgeon at the beginning. Let me back up. I know you've seen my scar, and you know I had a mastectomy. But before the mastectomy, I had a lumpectomy and radiation. Dr. Esposito was my original plastic surgeon. A year or so after my initial surgery, I had a complication. George was on call for my plastic surgeon, who was out of the country. It turned out that I had cellulitis and a cancer recurrence. That's when I had the mastectomy. George took care of my reconstruction after the mastectomy."

Geret studied her. Then he said, "You really cared for him, didn't you?"

Lacey felt uneasy. Thoughts of George began to rain on her happy mood. She looked at Geret and said, "I did. He was like the only family I had. I mean, he wasn't my family, but he was the closest thing I had to having someone like family. Most people who go through cancer have a support system. I had my friends, but I had no family. I felt connected to him, and I thought that he had the same connection to me. But he didn't."

They sat in silence for several minutes. Geret could see that Lacey was lost in thought. Finally, he said, "I'm sorry to open old wounds. I'm going to get going. It's late, anyway."

"It is late," Lacey said. "I guess the night has to end at some point."

Geret smiled at her and stood from the couch. He walked toward the front door, and Lacey stood and followed him.

"I'm sorry if I spoiled the mood tonight. We probably shouldn't have talked about old flames," Geret said with a half-smile.

"Well, it is what it is," Lacey said. Then she added, "We talked about them, but thankfully we don't have to go back to that time in our lives."

"That's right," he said. He reached out and took her hands in his and said, "I had a wonderful time tonight."

Lacey stared back up at him, and softly replied, "Me, too."

Without saying anything else, Geret gently pulled her toward him and kissed her tenderly. After the kiss, he pulled her closer. Lacey could feel the heat radiating from his body, as her head rested on his chest. He leaned in and gently kissed her forehead. He let go of her hands and slowly wrapped his arms around her lower back as he caressed her temple and cheek with his lips.

Lacey's stomach fluttered, and her knees started to weaken as he continued to give her slow, gentle kisses across her face. Then he kissed her cheek several times and said, "Sweet dreams. I'll be thinking about you."

Lacey looked up at him. Geret leaned in and pressed his lips gently to hers. Then he stepped slowly backward to open the door. "Good night," Geret whispered as he smiled and stepped outside. "Lock the door," he added, sounding paternal.

Lacey nodded and said, "Thank you. I had a great time."

Lacey closed the door and locked it. Then she leaned back on the door. The night had been wonderful, despite the fact that they had talked about Darla and George. She knew that sometimes it was necessary to air out the dirty laundry in order to move on with a new, clean load. She hadn't expected to feel so much pain with the mention of George's name, though. She still was not over him. *Will I ever move past my feelings for him?*

She focused her thoughts on Geret. She realized that if there was a man who could help her move past George, it was Geret. He had shown up in her life in some difficult and scary situations. He had been like a rock for her to cling to. Perhaps God had brought him to her as a source of strength and support. *But can I trust him for more?* She prayed, *Lord, show me what you have planned. Please help me to not get ahead of you but to wait for your good and perfect plan.*

Chapter Twenty-Seven

Over the next week, Lacey saw Geret at the hospital several times. It seemed that butterflies had just taken up residence in her stomach because they fluttered even at the thought of him. The man was gorgeous, and Lacey couldn't stop thinking about their date, his smile, his kisses, and the connection between them. Their time together had been fun and relaxing and just plain easy. She had been able to be herself, and it was refreshing. She believed he might just be different than the other men in her dating life. He outwardly cared for her without any pretense or forced effort. Rather than not being available for her, he had shown up during her most difficult struggles in Pocatello. He had shown her a consistency in his character that gave her confidence in who he was and how much he truly cared for her. The air in Lacey's world was starting to feel positive again, and she couldn't help but smile from her heart.

Friday morning, as Lacey walked to the preoperative area to see a patient she had scheduled for surgery, she expected to see Geret. He was usually somewhere near the preoperative area, surgery suite, or recovery room. For the last week, since their Saturday night date, he had appeared to be undoubtedly seeking her out, or so it had seemed. It's as if he knew where she would be, and he had made sure to put himself in her vicinity.

Lacey and Geret had shared several smiles and small talk at work, but they didn't want anyone to know they were dating. So they communicated by text, phone calls or after work hours. Geret had been thoughtful each day, making sure to text her several times a day to check in on her or just to let her know he was thinking about her. Geret was authentic, and it allowed Lacey to trust in his feelings for her. Tonight, he planned to pick her up at seven for dinner, and then they would play a few games of pool at her place. Lacey could hardly wait, and she could feel an extra bounce in her step.

Lacey spoke with her next surgery patient and reviewed the procedure with her again. As she stepped out of the patient's room, she caught a glimpse of Geret at the end of the hall. As she turned to walk in his direction, she stopped in her tracks. She noticed that he was leaning against the wall talking to a cute, surgery nurse. She had seen her before but couldn't remember her name. Lacey knew this nurse had a reputation for flirting, though.

Lacey stared at them for a moment. Geret's back was to Lacey, so she couldn't see his face. The nurse was smiling and obviously being flirtatious as she reached out and touched his chest. Lacey could feel her heart racing. Her stomach felt heavy. She saw Geret reach up for the nurse's wrist and take hold of it. Lacey couldn't watch them anymore. She turned away to leave the preoperative area.

Lacey walked into the locker room and went straight into a bathroom stall. Thankfully, no one was in the bathroom. She started to hyperventilate, and tears started to surface. Standing in the stall, she leaned back on the door. A tear rolled down her cheek as she tried to slow her breathing. *This can't be happening.* So far, every man she had loved ended up preferring someone else to her. Seeing Geret that close to the cute nurse seemed foreign to her. It seemed wrong and out of character for Geret. But she had seen it, with her own eyes.

How could I be so stupid? She shook her head and closed her eyes tightly. *Lord, I thought he was different from the others.* A wave of nausea came over her as she realized that she wouldn't see Geret anymore. She couldn't allow him any more time in her heart. Lacey shook off the vision of Geret and the cute nurse and pushed the wall up around her heart. *Never again.*

At home later that evening, Lacey lay listless on her bed. Her cell phone rang a few times, and it was Geret. She let the phone go to voicemail. She didn't know what to say to him because she felt angry and hurt. Her phone chirped.

Geret texted her, "Are you okay? Are we still on for tonight?"

Lacey finally texted him back with an excuse. She said, "Sorry, I've been feeling bad most of the day with a migraine. I'm in bed for the night. Talk to you later."

It wasn't just an excuse. Her head did hurt, along with her heart and soul. Lacey cried for several hours before eventually falling asleep.

Lacey avoided Geret on Saturday. He texted and called, but she ignored him and thought that eventually, he would get the hint. On Sunday, the doorbell rang. Lacey's heart leapt into her throat. She assumed Geret had come to inquire as to why she hadn't been responding to him. She didn't know what she would say.

Lacey opened the door and wanted to immediately slam it shut. It was Rusty.

"Hey," he said.

"Hi. How are you?" She responded with a flat expression.

"You look tired," he said.

Lacey stepped aside and waved him into the foyer out of the cold. As before, he didn't pick up on her disappointed look or her low energy.

Lacey felt repulsed as a wave of nausea came over her. She left the door slightly open, trying to signal to Rusty that he wasn't welcome. He didn't seem to have a clue that she had no interest in him. *That's because he only cares about himself,* she thought and then added, *like other men.*

"I'm about to leave," she said, which was a lie. Then she added, "What are you doing here?"

"Well, I just came by to see if you were free for lunch," he said, as if he expected her to be swept off her feet.

Before Lacey could utter her frustrated response, she heard another voice through the half-open front door.

"Sorry, Rusty, but she has plans with me today."

It was Geret. He gently pushed the door open and stepped into the foyer. Although Lacey was still angry with Geret, she was relieved to be rescued from Rusty. Despite her hurt feelings over Geret, her heart had still jumped in her chest at the sight of him.

"Oh, sorry. I didn't know you were seeing anyone, Lacey," Rusty said with a shocked look and a defeated tone.

"Um ... yeah, I am," Lacey said, feeling a little unsure of her response.

"Well, fine," Rusty said more defiantly. "I guess I'll be going."

Rusty left quickly and looked like a dog running off with his tail between his legs. Lacey was relieved to see him go. She was more relieved to know he wouldn't be dropping in for any more unsolicited visits.

Lacey closed the door behind Rusty to keep the cold out. She said, "I'm so tired of his visits. I appreciate what you did. I don't think he'll be stopping by anymore."

"He's a sore loser. But then again, I'd be mad to lose you too," Geret said with a big grin.

Lacey studied him without smiling. She wasn't sure how to proceed now that Geret was standing in her foyer.

Finally, Geret asked, "Can I come in for a minute?"

Lacey only nodded and then walked into the living room.

Geret removed his boots and followed her.

Lacey stood with her back to Geret. She didn't know what to say.

Geret walked up behind her and touched her shoulder. She pulled away and then turned toward him.

He asked, "What's going on, Lacey? You've been avoiding me."

She shook her head, as tears started to surface.

Geret saw her pain and moved toward her. "What is it? What happened?"

Lacey pursed her lips and stepped back. She said, "I just believed you were different."

Geret seemed puzzled, and asked, "What are you talking about?"

Lacey exhaled loudly and said, "I saw you with that cute nurse."

"What?" He asked.

Lacey could feel her anger building. She said with force, "Yesterday, in the preoperative area, I saw that cute nurse ... I can't remember her name ... I saw you talking to her. I saw her flirting with you. I saw her reach out and touch your chest."

Geret stood and looked at her for a moment trying to process what Lacey had seen. Then he looked up at the ceiling and pursed his lips. He exhaled, and said, "What you saw did happen."

"Why?" Lacey called out in pain. "Why would you capture my heart and make me have feelings for you and then go off and flirt with the first cute thing that comes along? Why would you do that? I thought I could trust you."

Geret shook his head and stepped toward her. He reached for her, but she pulled away. He said, "It's not what you think. Hear me out. You *can* trust me."

Lacey huffed out loud and crossed her arms. She asked, "So what did I really see, then? Tell me."

"That nurse is Tonya. She has a reputation for being a big flirt. She has also gotten in trouble twice for sexual harassment. When she reached for my chest, I grabbed her wrist to stop her. I pulled her into my office, told her I had to report this as another sexual harassment incident, and told her I would be talking to my boss. This was her last warning, and she knew it. I spent the day documenting the incident. I had witnesses to the incident also, and they had to do a write-up as well. Today, my boss fired her."

Lacey could feel her heart lighten as his story registered in her brain. She asked in a whisper, "You weren't flirting with her?"

He shook his head and replied, "No. The only woman I have eyes for is you."

Lacey suddenly felt tired. She hadn't slept well the night before, and the hours of crying and brooding had taken their toll. She looked at him with puppy dog eyes and said, "I'm sorry I doubted you."

Geret stepped toward her and pulled her into his arms. "Lady, you have no idea how much I care for you. I don't even see other women when they walk by me. You are on my mind night and day."

He pulled away from her to look at her. "Lacey, I'm in love with you."

Lacey leaned into him and rested her head on his chest. It felt good to be in his arms. Her heart felt relief from her pain, and she didn't want to ever leave his embrace. Her world felt right again. She looked up at him and said, "I'm in love with you, too."

Geret leaned in and kissed her gently and then with more passion. When they broke free of the kiss, he said, "Please don't ever doubt me. I will not lie to you, ever."

Lacey said, "I'm sorry. Okay, I won't doubt you." She could feel herself melting into him, as he held her for a while.

After a few minutes, Geret said, "I want to take you somewhere. Have you eaten lunch?"

"No, not yet," Lacey replied. "Where do you want to go?"

Geret squinted his eyes playfully and gave a flirtatious grin. He said, "You'll see. Trust me."

Lacey asked, "How long will we be gone?"

Geret smiled again. He asked, "How long have you got?" Then he added, "About three hours." Geret's eyes were dancing along with that flirtatious smile. She loved the softness and warmth she could see in his eyes.

"Okay," she said.

"Dress warm. We'll be outside for most of the time," he said.

Lacey put on her boots, coat, scarf, and gloves. Then she added a wool hat. She grabbed her purse, and they headed out.

Geret opened the truck door and helped her into the passenger seat.

"Where are we going?" Lacey asked as they pulled onto I-15 toward Idaho Falls.

He could tell she was uneasy, so he said, "I want to show you something in Idaho Falls, and then we can eat lunch."

Lacey relaxed and felt relieved to have things right between her and Geret again. A few minutes into the drive, she felt Geret take her hand. He intertwined his fingers with hers gently, and she turned to look at him. Their eyes locked for a few seconds, and she knew her heart would never be the same again.

Chapter Twenty-Eight

They were quiet for the first part of the forty-five-minute commute to Idaho Falls. Lacey was still reeling from the events of the past few days. The relief she felt from the truth had made her feel sleepy.

Half-way through the commute, Geret asked, "Have you found any more letters from your dad or clues at the house about your family?"

"Nothing new," Lacey replied. Then she added, "Did I ever tell you about the box I found in the built-in wardrobe in my bedroom?"

Geret glanced at her and shook his head. He said, "No, what did you find?"

Lacey told Geret about the box with her father's name on it and how it contained her baby shoes, the baby blankets and booties, and the record book of *Little Red Riding Hood*.

"I guess the blue blanket and booties had been for Luke?" He asked.

"Yes, that was my guess, too," she replied.

Then he chuckled and asked, "So you actually have a vinyl record of the story of *Little Red Riding Hood*?"

Lacey replied with a smile, "Yes, it's a book with the large vinyl record in a sleeve in the front of the book. The amazing thing is that I remember it."

He looked over at her with surprise. He asked, "You remember it?" Then he asked, "What year would that have been?"

"I think I was about two or three then, so 1982. I remember sitting in my daddy's lap and turning the pages with him while the record played the story."

He smiled widely, and Lacey could see his dimples. He said, "That's awesome, Lacey."

"Yeah, the memory is faint, but I do recall it. I just wish I could listen to that record again, though I don't even know if it will play. I wouldn't even know where to find a record player these days."

When they arrived in Idaho Falls, Geret pulled into a parking spot in the downtown area on the square in front of a deli. They walked in together and ordered sandwiches and drinks to go.

Lacey headed toward the truck, but Geret stopped her. "We're going this way," he said as he motioned to a park across the street. They sat down at a picnic table in the park and ate their lunch.

The park was small with several trees and a walking trail. Thankfully, the sun was out, and the breeze was light. The park was quiet and peaceful. Lacey could hear a few birds chirping in the nearby trees. She closed her eyes and inhaled. "I like it here," she said, and then added, "It's peaceful."

Geret replied, "I know. I came here a lot to think when I was going through that mess with Darla. It was comforting and gave me some peace. It was a place I could come to read my Bible and clear my mind and worries."

Lacey smiled at him. She was thankful he had brought her to this serene place.

"C'mon, let's walk," he said as he helped her up from the picnic table.

When they reached the walking path, Lacey could see down the hill by the path. There was a beautiful reservoir filled with flowing water that extended beyond the length of the walking trail. The breeze was bouncing off the surface of the water, causing occasional misty bursts in the air. "This is beautiful," she said softly.

"I knew you'd like it," he said, looking at her warmly. He held his gloved hand out to her, and she took it. He intertwined his fingers with hers. They walked down the trail, taking in the sunshine and the sound of the rushing water. A half mile down the trail, they turned around to make their way back to the truck.

On the way home, Geret took Lacey's hand in his. He turned to her, and asked, "Is there anyone in Pocatello who might have known your grandparents? I mean, maybe there is someone you could talk to who remembers them."

Lacey was touched by Geret's desire to help her learn more about her family. She replied, "I don't know. I hadn't really thought about it." A few minutes passed, and then she said, "I bet Drew's dad might have some information."

"Who's Drew?" Geret asked. Then he playfully added, "He's not a guy I need to be worried about, is he?"

Lacey chuckled and replied, "Silly. He's my attorney. His father, Paul, was my grandparents' attorney. He retired, and his son, Drew, took over the legal issues for the farm and farmhouse. I'm going to call Drew and see if I can get in touch with his dad. I don't know why I didn't think of it sooner. Thanks, Geret."

"I just asked a question," he said. He looked over at her and said, "I want you to find the answers you need. It has to be hard not knowing a lot about your family and your past."

When they reached her house, Geret walked her to the door. Lacey opened the door and turned toward Geret. "Do you want to come in for a while?" She asked.

"I actually have a really important errand to run," he replied.

"What kind of errand?" She asked.

"It's a surprise," he answered playfully.

"Oh, I see," she said, continuing the playful banter.

Geret leaned in closer to her and asked, "Will you spend this weekend with me?"

"Hmmm," she teased him. "Well, I'm not on call, so I could be persuaded to spend time with you."

Geret wrapped her in his arms and gave her a long, slow kiss. "See you soon," he said.

Chapter Twenty-Nine

On Monday morning, Lacey opened her office door and walked through the waiting room. Barbie was sitting at the reception desk. "Good morning, Barbie," Lacey said.

Barbie looked up from the desk and smiled. She replied, "Good morning, Dr. B. You're early today."

Lacey stopped at the desk and said, "Yeah, I need to make a phone call this morning. Plus, I have a lot of paperwork to catch up on. How was your weekend?"

Barbie smiled her wide smile and showed off her glistening braces. She replied, "I saw my grandkids this weekend. We did some baking and crafts. We had a great time. What did you do?"

Lacey raised her eyebrows and smiled. She said, "Oh, nothing much."

Barbie stood from the desk and followed Lacey to her office. She said, "Okay, Dr. B. I know that look. What did you do this weekend?"

Lacey smiled at her, as she hung her coat up. "Close the door and have a seat," she said while motioning Barbie to a chair in front of her desk.

"Oh my, this is going to be good. I just know it," Barbie said, sitting on the edge of the chair. "Okay, spill it," she added.

Lacey asked, "Can you keep a secret?"

Barbie wrinkled her forehead, and answered, "Of course. Now, tell me!"

Lacey chuckled at Barbie's impatience. She said, "I'm dating someone."

Barbie became wide-eyed and asked, "Who is it?"

Lacey replied, "I think you probably know."

Barbie looked like she might combust. She asked, "Is it Geret?"

Lacey smiled and nodded.

Barbie exploded with questions. She asked, "When did this happen? How long has it been going on? Is it serious?"

Lacey nodded and answered, "We went out officially right after Christmas, but he came over a few times before then. He fixed a leaky faucet for me. Then when I had the flu, he actually stayed overnight to care for me. This weekend, things became more serious when he told me he was in love with me."

Barbie just sat there with her mouth open. Her eyes looked like they might bug out. Finally, she said, "Remember that I told you he was a great catch? That says a lot about him that he took care of you when you were sick. That's so sweet that he's in love with you. Oh my gosh, this is so exciting!" She clasped her hands together, and added, "I knew you two would be perfect together. I'm so happy for you, Dr. B."

Lacey felt giddy. She replied, "Thank you. I feel really happy."

"Hopefully, finding happiness with Geret means you'll stay in Pocatello," Barbie said.

"Even without Geret, this place has really started to feel like home. The farmhouse holds a lot of memories of my family. It also has some unsolved mysteries."

Barbie tilted her head and looked at Lacey, "What do you mean?"

Lacey told Barbie about the box, her father's Bible, and her father's letters to her.

Barbie asked, "So, you're adopted, and you had a brother?"

Lacey nodded and said, "Apparently so."

Barbie asked, "Was there a third letter in the Bible?"

Lacey shook her head and replied, "No, I looked all through the Bible. I found nothing else."

Barbie was enamored with Lacey's unsolved mystery. She asked, "Why do you think your mom never told you?"

Lacey wrinkled her brow and exhaled loudly. She said, "I really don't know. I just don't understand."

Barbie asked, "So, if your biological mother died, whatever happened to your biological father?"

"I have no idea who he is or if he's still alive," Lacey replied.

Barbie excitedly said, "Dr. B, maybe you have biological siblings you don't know about."

Lacey replied, "It's definitely a mystery. I'm going to talk to my attorney's dad. His name is Paul Brown. He was my grandparents' attorney for years. He's retired now. I'm hoping he might have some answers for me. He is the one I'm going to call this morning."

Barbie stood from the chair and said, "Go ahead and call him. Maybe he can help. You've got me really curious now. Maybe I know your biological parents. Dr. B, you're actually a native of Pocatello. This is home for you. You belong here."

Lacey smiled and nodded. "I suppose that is true," she said.

Barbie opened the door and stepped out. She said, "I'm heading back to the desk. Make your call. Tell me what you find out." Then she leaned back in through the doorway, and said, "I'm so excited for you and Geret." Then she disappeared into the hallway.

Lacey picked up her office phone and dialed Paul Brown's number.

"Hello?" said a lady's voice.

"Hi, this is Lacey Bartlett. Is Mr. Brown available?" Lacey asked.

"Sure, just a moment," the lady said.

Within a few seconds, Lacey heard a man's voice, "Hello, this is Paul Brown."

"Hi, Mr. Brown. This is Lacey Bartlett." Lacey said.

Before Lacey could say anything else, Paul said, "Yes, Lacey, so nice to hear from you. I thought the world of your grandparents. Drew tells me you sold the acreage on the farm but that you're living in the farmhouse. How do you like it there?"

Lacey replied, "I love living in the house."

Paul asked, "How is your medical practice going? Drew told me you took the job at the Pocatello Regional Hospital."

Lacey replied, "It's going great. I've been very busy."

Paul asked, "So, how can I help you?"

Lacey cleared her throat. "Well, I asked Drew for your number. I have found a few discoveries at the farmhouse that have left me with questions. I wondered if you might be able to help me answer some of those questions."

Paul hesitated, and then asked, "Do you mean that you have questions about the house?"

Lacey answered, "No, my questions are about my grandparents and my dad. I found some letters my dad wrote to me." Lacey paused. She didn't want to talk about the letters over the phone.

Before she could say anything else, Paul said, "Why don't you stop over here at the house? I need to give you something."

"What do you have?" She asked.

"Why don't you just come over here at your convenience. I think I might be able to help you some," he said.

"That would be great," Lacey replied. She could feel her excitement building. Paul knew something. She asked, "May I stop over this evening after my office hours, maybe at six o'clock?"

Paul replied, "Sure, that would work fine." Then he added, "I'm not sure if what I have will answer all of your questions, but it may help."

After Lacey disconnected the call, she texted Geret and told him about her conversation with Paul.

He texted back right away, "Do you want me to go with you?"

She answered, "Would you, please?"

He texted, "When and where do I pick you up?"

Lacey smiled at his willingness to drop everything for her. She wrote back, "Can you pick me up at my house at five-thirty?"

"I'll be there," he texted back.

Chapter Thirty

Lacey and Geret were greeted by the housekeeper upon their arrival at Paul Brown's house. They were seated in the living room to wait for him. Paul lived on the outskirts of Pocatello in a small, ranch-style, custom-built home. His home backed up to the Snake River. The view of the river from the living room window was breath-taking, with the mountains as the backdrop.

Lacey waited with quiet anticipation for Paul to arrive. Geret sat beside her, holding her hand. They sat in silence until Paul finally made his appearance at the entrance to the living room from a back hallway. He walked slowly and leaned on a cane with every step. Lacey and Geret stood as Paul entered the room.

"Hi there. Please, sit down," he said. Geret walked over to him and helped him sit in a recliner. "Thank you, young man," he said.

Geret reached to shake Paul's hand after Paul was situated in the chair. "Mr. Brown, I'm Geret Blake. I'm Lacey's friend."

Lacey walked over to Paul and held out her hand. She said, "Hi, Mr. Brown. I'm Lacey. It's so nice to meet you."

Paul nodded at both of them and said, "Please, have a seat."

Lacey and Geret sat back down on the couch.

Paul looked at Lacey and said, "Your grandparents were some of my best friends. I felt honored to be associated with them in business for so many years. When your grand-mother became sick, she called me over to the farmhouse and had me write her will. She wanted you to have everything. Before I left that day, she handed me another letter. She told me that if you ever came to me asking questions about your family, I should give you this." He reached into his jacket pocket and pulled out an envelope. Handing it to Lacey he said, "I have no idea what this letter says. When you called me earlier today, I told you that I might be able to answer some of your questions, but I wasn't sure. I'm hoping that this letter will hold the answers you are searching for."

Lacey stood and retrieved the letter from Paul. She sat back down on the couch next to Geret. She hesitated to open the envelope and looked at Paul for a moment.

"Go ahead and open it if you want. If you have any questions after you read it, maybe I can give you additional answers," said Paul.

Lacey anxiously looked up at Geret.

He nodded at her and said, "Go ahead and read it. You've been hoping to find some answers."

Lacey carefully opened the envelope and unfolded the letter. She recognized the stationery. It was the same stationery her grandmother had written her previous letter on. Lacey read out loud, "It's dated, October 22, 2005 ..." then she read the rest to herself.

Dear Lacey,

I knew you would eventually be reading this letter. I knew you would grow into an intelligent, inquisitive woman, and I knew your heart would not stop searching until it had answers. I asked Paul Brown to give you this letter if you ever came to him with questions about your family.

You are adopted. Your mother made us promise to never tell you about your adoption. You have to know that she meant to protect you.

First and foremost, your mother didn't ever want you to feel that you had been unwanted or unloved. You were not discarded. Your birth mother, Hannah Clements, was only sixteen when she was pregnant with you and your brother, Luke. She never told your biological father, Lucas London, about you. She loved him very much. He had plans to go to college, and Hannah was not going to keep him from realizing his dreams. She broke things off with him when she found out she was pregnant. He was heartbroken, but she refused to see him. She even moved away for a while so he couldn't find her. Eventually, he believed she had really lost interest in him, and he went off to college. Lucas graduated with a Construction Management degree from ISU. He manages our farm, now that Grandpa has gone to Heaven. Lucas, who is your biological father, does not know about you. He is like a son to me, though. I hope you will want to meet him someday.

Hannah developed toxemia when she was pregnant with you and Luke. You were both born a few weeks early by an emergency Cesarean. Hannah had developed seizures and then had a stroke. Luke died just before delivery. The doctors said it was a cord accident. They said the umbilical cord had a blood clot in it, and it blocked oxygen to Luke.

Your mother could not conceive, because she was born without a uterus. She was ashamed of this and didn't want anyone to know. I think that is the other reason she wanted to keep the adoption a secret. Hannah picked your parents to adopt you through an adoption agency.

When you and Luke were born, Luke's death was unexpected and so sad. Your parents were rejoicing because of you and grieving because of the loss of Luke. Luke was named after his biological father, at Hannah's request. Hannah went into a coma during her seizures and died shortly after the Cesarean.

Your father wanted to tell you about the adoption. He wanted you to know how much he and your mother loved you and wanted you. He wanted you to know that Hannah didn't just discard you. She courageously gave you a life she couldn't provide for you. Your father once told me he had started writing a letter to you on each of your birthdays. If he did, there should be at least three letters. I looked everywhere for them, but I could not find them.

As you know, your father passed away when you were almost three. We told you he was killed in a car accident, because, again, your mother hoped to spare you from any additional pain. Truthfully, he died from a rare form of blood cancer, called non-Hodgkin's lymphoma. He passed away within two years. I still miss him so much.

Grandpa and I tried to keep your mother and you with us in Pocatello, but it was evident that your mother needed to go home to her parents in Kentucky. Your grandpa and I worked our fingers to the bone keeping the farm running. We didn't travel much because of the demands of the farm. We struggled for many years to build the farm up. Your grandpa was diagnosed with Alzheimer's when he was fifty-five and died a few years later. I developed rheumatoid arthritis, and I've been confined to a wheelchair for the last five years.

I hope you can forgive all of us for keeping secrets from you. Our intent was to protect you. I am praying for God's goodness in your life.

I love you so much,
Grandma

P.S. You should know that Lucas London has a son, your half-brother. His name is Samuel London.

Lacey just stared at the open letter in front of her, dumbfounded, then she said, "Let me read this to you." She read the letter out loud to them. When she was finished, she looked up at Paul as she tried to process the volume of information she had just read. Slowly she looked up at Geret and then at Paul. She said, "I have a brother."

Paul nodded. He said, "I know Samuel London. He is a little younger than you are, and he lives in Idaho Falls. He was always a good kid. I think he does remodeling on homes. He went into business with Lucas, your biological father, when he was a teenager. Then I'm pretty sure he went to ISU and studied architecture. After college, he worked with Lucas until Lucas was killed in that tragic construction accident. Recently, he went out on his own and started remodeling old buildings and historic homes. I'm pretty sure that he's married and has a couple children. I knew your biological father very well. He took care of the farmhouse and the farm acreage for years. He even lived in the farmhouse for a few years after your grandmother passed away."

Paul shook his head then he said, "I had no idea that Lucas was your biological father. I guess that makes Samuel your half-brother. Your grandmother had a heart of gold. I think she kept Lucas in the family because he really was family. I'll be darned."

Lacey's heart was racing. She couldn't believe she had a brother. Geret squeezed her hand gently. She looked up at him and then at Paul. She asked, "Do you have an address for Samuel?"

Paul thought for a minute. Then he said, "You know, I think Drew does. He did some legal work for him a few years ago. I remember because Drew was talking about Samuel's business. That's when I made the connection that he was Lucas' son."

Lacey stood from the couch, and then Geret stood with her. She said, "Mr. Brown, thank you for sharing this letter with me."

Paul replied, "You're welcome. I would stand if I was stronger and lead you out, but I should probably stay put."

Lacey smiled. She replied, "We can find our way out. I really appreciate the information you've given me."

As Lacey and Geret started to walk out, Paul said, "You know, Lacey, your grandmother would have been so proud of you. I hope you really understand how much she loved you."

"I do," she replied, nodding.

Lacey and Geret sat in silence after climbing into the cab of his truck. She looked at him and said, "I can't believe this."

He took her hand in his, and said, "Does it make you feel better to have those answers?"

She smiled at him and nodded. She said, "Yes, of course. I just think I'm in shock. I mean, part of me hoped I might have a sibling or that I might be able to meet my biological father. I just didn't expect that it would become a reality. I really have a brother."

Geret nodded.

Lacey looked at him and asked, "If I go find him, how do you think he will react to the knowledge that he has a long-lost, half-sister?"

"Only one way to find out," he replied.

Chapter Thirty-One

Lacey spent the rest of that week busy in the office. She told Barbie all that she had learned about her family. Barbie was thrilled to learn that Lacey had a half-brother. The mystery had been solved for Lacey, but there was still one thing she had to do. She needed to go meet Samuel.

On Friday night after work, Lacey sat on her couch waiting for Geret to arrive. The gas fireplace hummed, and the heat from it was comforting. She stared at the piece of paper in front of her on the coffee table. Samuel's address was written on the paper. She hadn't decided how to approach Samuel with the news that he had a sister. Although she wanted to meet him, she felt an inner conflict about how divulging that information to him might change her life and his. She was nervous about it. *What if he didn't want to have a sister? What if he rejects me? What if he doesn't believe me?*

As she contemplated Samuel's possible reactions, there was a knock on the door. *There's Geret.* She stood and walked to the door, still lost in thought. Lacey opened the door. Her breath caught in her throat, and she stared at her visitor, dumbfounded. It was George.

"Hey Beautiful," George said.

Lacey just looked at him, not believing that he was standing there. His eyes sparkled, but she sensed that he was nervous. She felt her heart begin to melt at the sight of him. At the same time, she also felt old heartache resurfacing.

"G-George. What are you doing here?" She finally blurted out.

"Hi. I'm sorry to surprise you like this. I'm just so glad I found you," replied George.

Lacey stood still, feeling paralyzed and continued to stare at him.

George asked, "May I come in and talk to you?"

She motioned for him to step in out of the cold and closed the door behind him.

George stood inside the foyer looking at her. He said, "I'm sorry to surprise you this way. I didn't know exactly what I should do."

Lacey's heart was racing. "Uh ... come in."

She stepped into the living room, and George followed her. He took his coat off and laid it on the couch.

Lacey asked him, again, "George, why are you here?"

George looked around the house and asked, "Why are you living in an old farmhouse?"

"This home belonged to my grandparents. I lived here for the first few years of my life," she replied.

"I didn't know you were born in Idaho," he said.

She replied, "There is a lot you don't know about me."

George said, "Fair enough. Can we sit down?"

Lacey motioned to the couch, but she remained standing by the foyer door. She watched him walk over to the couch. He still looked good, and it made her heart ache. His hair was still as black and smooth as she remembered. He was wearing a black Henley with the sleeves pushed up on his forearms, faded jeans, and black boots. He looked better than she remembered. George sat down on the couch, but Lacey remained standing.

George looked up at her with a pleading look and asked, "Will you please sit with me?"

Lacey hesitated but then nodded and plopped down on the other end of the couch. She couldn't understand how he could just show up like this after all that had happened between them. She wondered how he had found her in Idaho. *Isn't he married?*

George looked at her and said, "I know that the last time we spoke, our conversation did not end well. I came here to tell you that I did not get married." He paused to let his words sink in, and then he continued, "My feelings for you were stronger than I realized. When we ended our call that night, something happened in me. I tried to shrug it off as cold feet. But when you moved across the country, you took a piece of me with you. It didn't take me long to realize that I'd made a big mistake."

Lacey sat quietly, pondering George's words. Then she said, "I don't know what to say. I'm shocked that you're here. I thought you were married. It's been months since I've seen or heard from you. A lot has changed since the last time we spoke."

George said, "I understand that you're upset. I expected that. I would feel the same way if you did this to me. I get it. Be upset, but please give me a chance to show you my change of heart."

Lacey crossed her arms in front of her chest. She asked, "Why didn't you just call or text me? Why would you just show up at my house?"

George cocked his head to one side and frowned, "Do you really think you would have answered me? Do you think you would have agreed to let me come see you? I knew this was my only hope of seeing you and talking to you again."

He was right, and Lacey knew it. There was no way she would have voluntarily opened a time slot in her day for him, not after he had chosen another woman over her.

Lacey shook her head to clear it. "George," she said, "I need to think about this. I'm really lost for words right now. It's not fair for you to just show up on my doorstep months after you were supposedly married and tell me that you didn't marry her because you care for me."

Without warning, tears started to flow as Lacey felt overwhelmed with emotions. She felt heartache, anger, hope, frustration, memories of past betrayal, and heartache all come alive in her at once.

George scooted toward her and wrapped his arms around her. He said, "I'm so sorry. If I could take back that day on the phone, I would. But I can't, and I need you to please forgive me. Give me a chance to show you that I care for you. I think I'm in love with you."

Lacey wanted to push him away at first. He had hurt her deeply. She thought she was over him, but as he held onto her, her old feelings of love for him returned. She had missed him. She sobbed as he held her.

After several minutes, Lacey pushed away from him and said, "I need to wash my face."

George let her go, reluctantly. She could see the sorrow in his face, but she didn't think he truly understood how much he had hurt her or how long she had suffered.

Lacey went to the bathroom and looked in the mirror. Her face was red and swollen from crying. She leaned down and splashed cold water on her face. This visit from George, and his words, seemed surreal. She had dreamed many times of the day he would return to her and confess his love for her. She had just never imagined that it would actually happen. Now that it had happened, she didn't know how to process it. She had fallen in love with Geret. When that happened, she had stopped thinking about George. She had stopped hurting, and she had stopped hoping to be loved back. This situation should be a no-brainer for her now. So why was her heart aching again?

As she patted her skin dry with a towel, she heard George talking to someone. Lacey suddenly remembered Geret was supposed to be stopping by at any minute. Lacey ran down the hallway toward the front door. George had closed the door and was walking into the living room with a medium-sized box.

"Who was that?" Lacey asked.

"I believe he said his name was Geret. He wanted me to give this box to you. I guess he had a delivery," George replied.

Lacey darted to the window. She spotted Geret's truck at the end of her driveway. He was leaving. Lacey could feel her heart yearning for Geret. *What must he think?*

"George, you need to leave," she said.

He nodded and walked over to her. "I will go. I understand how hard this is for you."

Lacey looked at him, "Do you? Do you really understand how you are messing with my feelings? With my life?" She paused. Then she said, "I'm not sure what you were thinking. So much time has passed. You have a plastic surgery practice in Louisville. I have my own patients in Pocatello. Were you going to be willing to move here if things worked out for us?"

He looked down, "I'm sorry." George put his coat on. He said, "I honestly didn't have a plan. I just knew I had to come talk to you. I didn't think this out all the way." Then he looked up at her and said, "But you know how matters of the heart can make people do crazy things. I just know that when I realized I was in love with you, I had to come tell you. Please don't fault me for that."

Lacey exhaled and looked up at him. Tears were collecting in her eyes again.

George walked toward the front door and then turned to her. He said, "I will be staying at the Courtyard Marriott here in town until Tuesday. I won't bother you anymore. If you decide you want to talk some more, please come see me. It may be that I'm too late to make things right. In that case, if I don't hear from you, then I'll leave quietly on Tuesday. I just hope you'll give us a chance."

Lacey stood, with her eyes focused on the floor. She nodded without looking at him.

George leaned toward her and wrapped his arms around her and then kissed each of her cheeks. He said, "Don't give up on me, Beautiful."

Chapter Thirty-Two

As soon as George was gone, Lacey texted Geret. He didn't respond. She knew Geret had figured out that the man who answered her front door was George. He had seen the photograph of her and George from graduation. She felt panicked. She had to talk to Geret.

Lacey threw on her coat and boots, grabbed her purse, and drove to Geret's house. Though she had never been to his house, she knew the address. Upon arrival at the address, she saw Geret's truck in the driveway and knew it was his house.

Lacey rang the doorbell, but there was no answer. The lights were on inside and his truck was there, so he had to be home. She wondered if he wasn't answering on purpose because of his exchange with George. She peeked through the small door window, but she couldn't see him. Then she heard what sounded like an ax chopping wood coming from his backyard. She walked around the side of the house to the back. Sure enough, Geret was chopping firewood in the backyard.

Lacey stopped to stare at him for a minute. He was working furiously, as if he was trying to work out some frustration. She waited for him to come to a stopping point. Then, she yelled out, "Geret!"

He turned to look at her and did a double take. She opened the gate and let herself into the fenced backyard.

"Hey," he said.

"Hi," she replied. The air was cold, and she could see their breath as they spoke. They stared at each other for a few awkward minutes, and finally, Lacey said, "I know you just came by the house."

"I did. That was the plan, right?" He asked, throwing the chopped logs into a pile.

"Yes, it was. I'm sorry you were greeted by George at the door. It's not what you think," she said.

"You don't owe me an explanation," he said as he continued to pile the chopped logs. Then he paused and asked, "Did you get the box I asked him to give to you?"

Lacey felt frustrated. She answered, "Yes, but I haven't opened it yet ... Geret, I *do* owe you an explanation. Do you think we could go inside and talk for a few minutes?"

Geret nodded. He said, "Sure." He put the ax down and leaned it against a tree stump.

Once inside, Geret wouldn't look at her. He casually asked, "I'm going to make some coffee. Do you want a cup?"

"No, thank you," she replied. She walked over to stand beside him and said, "Geret, I haven't spoken to George since I moved to Pocatello. Today, he just showed up at my front door. When I answered the door, I expected to see you. I was shocked."

Geret poured a cup of coffee. Without looking up, he asked, "What did he want?"

Lacey exhaled, "Well, he—"

Geret looked up at her and said, "He wants you back. Doesn't he?"

Lacey could see the pained look in his face. She pursed her lips, and replied, "Well, pretty much. He told me he made a mistake."

Geret shook his head, "He did make a mistake. He should've never let you go."

Geret took a sip of his coffee. Then he motioned to the kitchen table, and he and Lacey sat down. He took a few more sips and set his cup down. He looked at her and asked, "I take it he didn't get married?"

Lacey shook her head no.

Geret asked, "So, he wants to marry you?"

Lacey closed her eyes for a second and then opened them. She sighed and replied, "I don't really know what he wants. He just showed up at my door, uninvited, telling me he's in love with me. He said he didn't realize it until he started planning his wedding."

Geret was quiet and stared at her. Then he asked, "Do you still love him?"

Lacey covered her face with her hands and then rubbed her eyes. Tears started to form. She said, "Geret, I don't know. When I saw him, a lot of feelings that I thought I had buried rushed back to the surface. My heart is feeling tossed around in confusion."

Geret leaned forward with his elbows on the table and with a stoic expression said, "Matters of the heart are so tricky. Just when you think you have them all figured out, something happens to make you realize you don't."

A tear escaped and ran down Lacey's cheek. She said, "You have to know how much I care about you. I'm in love with you."

Geret remained quiet and stared at her intensely. Then he said, "But—"

Lacey shook her head and said, "I'm so tired. There have been so many different things coming at me lately. It's hard to process them all. I feel like I'm reeling emotionally. I need some time to sort through all of this."

Geret ran his fingers through his hair before he leaned across the kitchen table. He took Lacey's hands in his and looked into her eyes. He said, "Lacey, I know you've had a lot dumped on you in a short period of time. It's not fair to you. I've seen you be courageous and bold, and I've seen your gentle heart and spirit be almost broken. All I can tell you is that God wants the very best for you. Like your dad's letters said, ask God for what you need. Trust Him to show you what He wants for you. He will come through for you."

Then he paused for a moment and said, "I think it's important for you to know something about me. I know we have just started to see each other; but with George showing up in your life again, you have expressed the need for time and patience, so you can work through your feelings. To be fair to you, I need to also tell you what I need."

Lacey sat quietly, looking at him. She nodded, waiting for him to continue.

Geret's face remained intense as he spoke, "You may wonder why I haven't dated anyone since Darla."

Lacey nodded.

Garet said, "The thing is, I'm looking for a special kind of love, and it's hard to find. My mom used to call it covenant love. It makes me think of that painting hanging in your kitchen, the *covenant bouquet*. It's love with a lifetime promise ... like your grandpa gave your grandma. It's the kind of love I want to give, but it's also the kind of love I need in return." Geret took a sip of his coffee and continued, "When Darla and I dated for over three years, I was convinced she loved me because she had put the time in. What I discovered is that time and intent don't always translate to faithfulness of the heart. Somewhere along our life together, Darla decided that I wasn't enough for her. She decided that she didn't care for our commitment enough to stay the course. I'm looking for someone who wants to share her life with me completely in a committed relationship. I want covenant love. It's a love that is a promise that, as a couple, neither of us will ever leave or give up when things get tough and that we will always be enough for each other."

Lacey could relate to Geret's words because they resonated with her soul. She had longed for a family for years. She, too, yearned for a loving and committed relationship. She choked back a tear and said, "That's beautiful. Thank you for sharing that with me. I understand."

He nodded and said, "I will wait for you because I think we can share that kind of love." He paused, and then said, "You just have to decide what you want."

Lacey nodded slowly and pursed her lips. It seemed ironic to hear those words. Not even a year previous, she had said something similar to George.

As Lacey stood up, Geret stood and wrapped his arms around her. He kissed her forehead and then pulled back to look at her. He said, "Take your time. I'm not going anywhere. I love you, and I'll wait."

Lacey nodded, as she sniffled and wiped a tear from her cheek.

Geret walked her to her SUV and watched her as she drove off.

Lacey arrived home and parked under the carport. The house felt cold, and Lacey shivered when she walked into the kitchen. She went straight to the thermostat and bumped it up to 72. Then she turned on the gas fireplace switch in the living room. *Central heating will have to be installed before next winter*, she thought.

Lacey walked into her bedroom and changed into her flannel pajamas. She stepped into her slippers and then put her robe on over her pajamas. *This ought to help me stay warm.* She proceeded to the kitchen and made herself a cup of hot tea. As her tea steeped, she leaned on the kitchen counter and thought about her life. So much had happened in her little over three decades of life. So much had changed. She had been through a divorce, medical school, breast cancer, residency training, a broken heart, a move to Pocatello, and the discovery of years of hidden secrets about her family. In her job, she had cared for a rural population of patients, and she had been required to use her skills in challenging surgical cases.

Lacey took her tea to the living room and sat on the couch near the fire. Her thoughts drifted to George. Had he really come all the way to Pocatello just to tell her he had made a mistake? She had adored this man for years. He had cared for her during a difficult time in her life. She had been afraid for her life during those years. Even though he said he was in love with her, she still found it hard to believe. Despite his words, there was a missing link between his words and his actions.

Geret's face came to her mind. She smiled, and her heart swelled with love. She loved what he had said about covenant love. She was amazed at how his words seemed to come straight from his heart. He wasn't afraid to say what he was really feeling. She closed her eyes, and she could hear him saying, "I love you." This man was special to her, and she was certain she felt love for him, too. But seeing George brought back memories of what they had been through. So much of her past pain, feelings, and longings had just been dumped back onto the surface of her heart. She wasn't sure if her heart could absorb such a load of emotions.

Lacey exhaled loudly shaking her head. She was exhausted. She prayed out loud, "Lord, I need your guidance. Why did George come back now? What does this mean? Does it mean anything? I'm in love with Geret. He's such a good man. Things were going so well, and I felt happy. Why did George have to come back into my life? Lord, I don't know what to do. Please show me."

Chapter Thirty-Three

On Monday afternoon, Lacey sat in her office finishing her charting. Her day had been filled with patients, phone calls, and a C-section at noon. She was thankful for the flurry of activity since it gave her a distraction from her thoughts.

At four o'clock, Barbie stood in her office doorway with a bouquet of a dozen red roses. She set them on Lacey's desk. She said, "Dr. B, somebody loves you."

Lacey looked up in surprise at the sight of the beautiful roses. She took the card while Barbie sat down in a chair across from her desk. Lacey opened the card. It read, *Beautiful roses for my beautiful lady. Love, George.*

Barbie grinned. She asked, "Are they from Geret?"

Lacey looked up from the note at Barbie. She pursed her lips and replied, "No. They are from George."

Barbie looked confused. "Who's George?"

Lacey exhaled and asked, "Do you have a few minutes?"

Barbie nodded at Lacey with wide eyes, as if she couldn't wait to hear the story. "Please, tell me. I've got all day."

Lacey proceeded to tell Barbie her story. She started with her first meeting with George and then ran through all the details until her move to Pocatello. Barbie's eyes widened with every detail. She was enthralled with the story. Then Lacey told her about George showing up at her door over the weekend.

"What did he want? Does he want to marry you?" She asked covering her open mouth, as if in shock.

Lacey replied, "I don't know exactly what he wants. He just told me he couldn't marry the other woman because he realized he was in love with me. He says he showed up at my door because love makes people do crazy things."

"What are you going to do? Does Geret know?" Barbie asked.

Lacey closed her eyes and exhaled loudly. She looked down at the floor. She said, "He knows. George actually answered the door when Geret came over. Geret knew it was George because he had seen a photograph of us together."

Barbie just stared at Lacey with her mouth gaping open.

Lacey nodded. She said, "I know. Geret left, and I went to his house after George left. I told Geret I felt confused."

Barbie asked, "What are you going to do? I mean, if you work things out with George, will you move back to Kentucky?"

Lacey replied, "I don't know. I really haven't thought that far. I'm still trying to get past the shock of the situation. I really don't want to leave. I feel like Pocatello is my home. I'm finally discovering my family roots, and I love the farm-house."

Barbie asked, "What about Geret?"

Lacey said, "I think this breaks Geret's heart. He is such a good man with such a big heart. He told me he loves me, and he wants me to take all the time I need."

"He told you he loves you?" Barbie asked with a surprised look.

"Yes, he told me last night," Lacey replied.

Barbie said, "I think that's a big step for Geret. He hasn't dated anyone since Darla. He must really care for you." Then she paused and added, "I don't know what kind of guy George is, but I know that Geret is a great guy. He is a stand-up kind of guy who will be true to his word. That kind of guy is hard to find."

Lacey smiled. She replied, "I know. He is wonderful. I think I just have to work through some things."

Barbie nodded. She said, "Well, if I can help in any way let me know." She stood and walked to the doorway. Then she turned and said, "I'll say a prayer for ya."

Lacey smiled and said, "Thanks, Barbie. You're the best. I know everything will work out."

At home that night, Lacey sat on her couch and sipped on a cup of hot tea. She had changed into her pajamas and had her feet stretched out on the couch. The fireplace was humming and warming the room. Lacey missed Geret. She had become accustomed to talking and texting with him every day over the last month and a half. It felt wrong to not talk to him. She had hoped to see him during the C-section that afternoon, but he was nowhere to be found. Her days didn't feel right without him. She felt like a silly, happy schoolgirl when she remembered that he told her he loved her. She smiled.

George texted her a couple of times that day to tell her he was thinking about her. Lacey texted him back once to thank him for the flowers. Her memories with George had been flooding her mind intermittently that day. However, it struck her how the memories only brought heaviness to her heart. There was no joy, only sadness, in those memories. She had gone through a hard time in her life with him, and he had seemed like the closest thing to family at the time. Her residency graduation night had really been the only time with him that she had felt special to him, as a woman. Granted, they had shared a lot of interactions in their past, but now that she thought about it, most of them were centered around their doctor-patient relationship. She closed her eyes and wondered, *Why do I feel so confused?*

Lacey glanced around her living room. As she did, she caught a glimpse of a box on the floor. Then she remembered that Geret dropped it off when George had answered the door. She walked over to the box and moved it to the coffee table. She retrieved a pair of scissors from her office and opened the box.

She reached into the box and pulled out another box. When she recognized what it was, tears immediately filled her eyes, and she smiled. It was a record player. Geret had found a record player and bought it for her so she could listen to her childhood story of *Little Red Riding Hood.* His gift overwhelmed her so much that she had to sit down. She closed her eyes and could feel her heart aching for Geret. This man understood her. He had looked into her soul, and he cared about what she needed.

Lacey wiped her eyes and then walked to her bedroom. She pulled the box with her dad's name on it from the wardrobe. She retrieved the record story of *Little Red Riding Hood* and returned to the living room. She plugged in the record player and turned it on. Once she put the record on the player, the story began to play. Lacey sat on the couch thumbing through the story page by page while the record told the story. The moment was so heartwarming and sentimental for her. She could almost imagine being a young girl again, sitting in her father's lap, thumbing through the pages and listening to the story with him. The story ended, and Lacey closed the last page. She began to sob. Geret had done something very special for her.

After a few moments, she went to replace the record in the cover of the book. As she tried to replace it, she couldn't push it in all the way. Something was in the way. She reached inside the cover and felt a piece of paper. She pulled it out and was surprised to see that it was a yellow folded steno notepaper. Her heart began to race as she unfolded the note. *Is this from Daddy?* She read:

My Dearest Lacey Lou,

Today we celebrated your second birthday. You are my beautiful baby girl, yet you're growing up so fast. Your birthday party was fun, and I could tell how much you loved your record book of Little Red Riding Hood. We must have listened to the story nearly a dozen times.

My time is running out, and so I write this letter with a heavy heart. I won't be sending you any more letters on your birthdays, but know that I'm always with you. Part of me questions God about my illness. Why would He take me away from this life and from you so soon? I feel cheated. I already miss you so much.

I can't help but worry about you. You are young still, and you have so much life to live with many more lessons to learn. I write this final letter to tell you how much I will always love you.

Since I won't be there to advise you while you grow up, I want to pass on some of the wisdom I have learned. I hope this will help you. You will find that navigating through this life can be hard. You will have a lot of highs and lows. The older you become; the more responsibility you'll have thrown at you. There are three important lessons I want to leave with you.

First, always keep God first in everything you do. He is your anchor, your guide, your confidant, and your protector. Always go to God for help and direction first. He has a plan for you, and He will help you.

Second, become an independent woman. Set goals for your future career, for the type of friends you want, and for your future family. Be able to provide for yourself, strive for excellence in whatever work you do, and plan as best as you can for what you want in your future.

And last, when it is time, ask God to choose a husband for you. A man of God's choosing will be willing to commit to you. He will be able to make a covenant of love with you. That's the kind of love that sticks when life gets too hard. Your mom and I have this. It's love with a commitment to stay when it seems easier to leave. It's the kind of love God has for you. He will never leave you. Wait for a covenant love like that.

Please know that I miss you every day, and I'm trusting God to care for you. I know He will. I will see you again in Heaven, and I look forward to that day.

All my love,
Daddy

Lacey laid the letter on the coffee table. She stared at it for several minutes. Her father had used the same term Geret had used, *covenant love.* It was as if he had talked to Geret. Her father's words gave her peace. She felt as if he had come from the grave to tell her what she needed to hear. Her heart was overwhelmed with her father's love, and she could feel God's arms wrap around her. *This is an answered prayer.*

Lacey stood from the couch. She felt sudden clarity and knew what she had to do.

Chapter Thirty-Four

On Tuesday afternoon, Geret drove home from the hospital. After bringing some firewood inside, he started a fire in the wood-burning stove. He brewed a fresh pot of coffee, poured a cup, and then settled onto the couch beside the warm stove. It was cold outside, and it had snowed another five inches. He felt a cold chill and took a sip of the hot coffee. He felt the warmth of the coffee in his stomach.

Geret sat in silence trying to warm himself by the stove. He had hoped to see Lacey that day in surgery, but she hadn't scheduled any cases. He missed her and thought back to their last conversation, playing it over and over in his mind. His words to her had been carefully chosen, and he hoped that she would be able to accept what he had told her. Part of him wanted to call her now and give in to any demands she wanted to make, but he knew he couldn't go back to a situation like he had with Darla. He had to stick to his resolve and believe that love would find its way back to him.

Sadness fell over his heart as he realized he might lose her. He didn't know how strong George's pull was on her heart, but he wasn't going to underestimate it. Lacey had spent a lot of time with George. She had bonded with him during a difficult time in her life. Geret knew that George still had a firm grip on her heart.

Geret looked upward and prayed silently. *Lord, give Lacey wisdom and strength. Please be with her and protect her.*

I love her. Then he added, *Please give me strength to get through whatever happens between us.* Geret exhaled and stood to walk toward the kitchen.

Geret was looking in the pantry for something to eat when he heard a knock at the front door. He looked at his watch. It was nearly eight o'clock. He furrowed his brow, wondering who might be visiting this late. He walked to the door and opened it. Lacey was standing on his snow-covered front porch holding a bouquet of flowers. Geret's heart leapt in his chest. He was both excited and nervous to see her.

Lacey smiled at him and said, "Hi."

Geret smiled an uncertain smile and stepped back to let her in. He replied, "Hi, come in."

Lacey stepped in and stomped the snow off her boots onto the entry rug. She handed Geret the flowers and asked, "Will you hold these, please?"

Geret took them from her, and Lacey removed her boots and her coat. Geret disappeared into the kitchen, and Lacey followed him. He placed the bouquet of flowers on the kitchen table.

"It's freezing today. The wind gusts went right through me," she said, trying to make conversation.

Geret stared at her, unsure what to say. Finally, he asked, "Can I get you something?"

She shook her head no. Her eyes began to water as she said, "I've missed you."

Geret looked at her with sad eyes and replied almost in a whisper, "I've missed you, too."

They stood in silence.

Geret broke the silence after a few minutes, and asked, "Did you want to talk about something?"

Lacey nodded. She said, "George is on his way back to Kentucky."

Geret's face lightened upon hearing Lacey's words. He replied, "I take it he didn't like the cold, Idaho climate?"

Lacey half-smiled and said, "Yeah something like that."

Another moment of silence passed between them. Geret eyed the flowers and asked, "Why are you carrying flowers with you?"

Lacey grinned. She replied, "I brought them for you."

"Why?" He asked.

Lacey leaned toward the flowers and carefully cupped a red rose in her hand. She asked, "Did you know that the red rose is considered the ultimate gift given to express love?"

Geret raised an eyebrow. He answered, "Makes sense."

Then Lacey cupped a daisy in her hand gently. She said, "The daisy means *true love*."

Geret nodded and half-smiled.

Lacey turned the bouquet and pointed toward a white flower. She said, "This is a tree peony. It represents *honor and beauty*."

Geret nodded again.

Lacey pointed to one of the clusters of blue flowers. She said, "These little guys are forget-me-nots. They represent a *connection that lasts through a lifetime*."

Geret stared at Lacey.

Lacey picked up a few sprigs of the baby's breath and pulled them out of the bouquet. She said, "These dainty flowers represent *the power of the Holy Spirit in an everlasting love*."

Geret's eyes watered as he stepped toward Lacey. He asked, "Why are you telling me this?"

Lacey looked up at him. She said, "Geret, I want to share a covenant love with you."

Geret smiled as a tear escaped his eye. He wrapped his arms around her and gazed into her eyes. He kissed her tenderly. Then he looked at her and said, "You could have just told me you wanted to be with me. You didn't have to bring me flowers. I should be the one getting you flowers."

She smiled and said, "No, you don't understand."

He furrowed his brows in confusion and said, "What do you mean?"

Lacey's eyes watered as she tried to hold back tears. She replied, "You bought me that wonderful record player. I listened to the story of *Little Red Riding Hood*. I reveled in the memory of listening to the story with my father. It was so special to me."

Geret nodded and smiled. He said, "I'm so happy it made you happy. That was my intent." Then he paused and added, "But what does that have to do with the flowers?"

Lacey grinned and sniffled. She said, "Well, when I went to replace the record back in its cover, I couldn't get it to slide in, because there was something blocking it. I reached in and found my father's third letter to me."

Geret raised his eyebrows in surprise and smiled. "What did it say?"

Lacey continued, "He gave me some wisdom for living. One of the most important things he told me was that I needed to let God choose a husband for me. He said I would know I'd found the right man, when that man would offer me a covenant of love."

Geret reached for her. His eyes filled with tears.

Lacey leaned into him and placed her hand on his cheek. She wiped a tear from his face. Then she said, "Those are the flowers from my grandmother's painting. I wanted to bring you a covenant bouquet."

Geret engulfed Lacey in his arms. He kissed her gently and then more passionately. Then he looked at her as the corners of his mouth turned upward. He asked, "So, you realize this covenant bouquet is a bridal bouquet, right?"

Lacey nodded.

He grinned and playfully asked, "Are you asking me to marry you?"

Lacey chuckled. Then she looked at him seriously and nodded. She said, "Yes."

Geret leaned over to the bouquet. He picked out a rose and handed it to her. He said, "I love you."

Lacey replied, "I love you, too."

Then he picked out a daisy and handed it to her. He said, "You are my true love."

Lacey held the two flowers and looked at him with an inquisitive smile.

Geret picked a white peony and a forget-me-not from the bouquet and handed them to Lacey. He said, "I will honor you and spend the rest of my life with you."

Lastly, he pulled a sprig of baby's breath from the bouquet and handed it to Lacey. He said, "I promise to love you with an everlasting love and to always keep God at the center of our relationship."

Epilogue

The weather in Pocatello was beautiful in June that year. The mountains were covered with hues of green, brown, red, and purple. The snow caps were a sight to see in the middle of eighty-degree days. Lacey inhaled the warm breeze and the scents of summer.

Jen and Katy had arrived in Pocatello two days before the wedding. They were thrilled to be Lacey's matrons of honor. The three girls spent a day at the spa and had lunch. They had so much to catch up on.

Back in February, Lacey and Geret had gone to meet Samuel. Samuel accepted her with open arms. Lacey had been surprised at how he teared up at the news and embraced her for a long time. He was overjoyed that he had a sister. Lacey recalled spending at least three hours with Samuel that day. They had gone through the letters over and over. They talked about their relatives, their childhoods, and their memories. Samuel was married to Lauren, and they had two children, Lucas, age six, and Leyton, age four. Since that day, Lacey and Geret had visited Samuel and his family every weekend for Sunday dinner.

In late February, Geret surprised Lacey with a one-carat princess-cut diamond ring. He proposed to her on bended knee in the middle of her living room. Although he had accepted her proposal over the covenant bouquet, he had insisted that it was important for him, as a man, to be the one to ask. Lacey rolled her eyes and smiled at the memory.

Now, Lacey stood at the edge of the rolled-out white carpet. The sun was just starting to set. She looked toward her destination, and locked eyes with Geret, who stood there at the other end of the carpet. He was dressed in a black tuxedo, and oh, did he look fine. His smile melted her heart. *Thank you for this moment, Lord. You have provided for me. I am so grateful.*

Samuel stood next to Geret as his best man. Two of Geret's friends stood next to Samuel as Geret's groomsmen. Little Lucas stood beside his father holding a pillow with the rings on it. The pastor stood under the wedding arch. The arch was decorated with red roses, daisies, white peonies, blue forget-me-nots, and baby's breath. *Covenant love,* Lacey thought, and she smiled to herself. She looked down at her bridal bouquet and observed all of the same flowers. Her heart smiled.

She looked up again and saw Jen and Katy standing on the left side of the pastor. They were wearing light blue dresses in the same shade as the blue forget-me-nots. Next to them stood Barbie, in the same colored dress. She was smiling so big, Lacey could see the sun reflecting on her braces. Lacey's heart swelled at the beautiful scenery. This was her family.

Leyton walked down the aisle dropping red rose petals. Lacey chuckled at Leyton's cuteness. Leyton stopped when she got to her mother's row and sat down next to Lauren. That hadn't been the plan, but it was adorable.

There were only a few friends in attendance. Most of these people were people Lacey and Geret worked with. Drew Brown and his wife were also in attendance. They had brought Drew's father, Mr. Paul Brown, and he sat next to Drew's wife.

The bridal march sounded from the string quartet that was playing to the side. Lacey took a deep breath. It was time. She paused for a moment as she thought of her mother and father. Her mother would have wanted to be here to see her in her wedding gown. Lacey wore an old blue topaz flower pendant on her necklace. Her mother had given it to her before she passed away. She imagined seeing her mother sitting up in the front row, turning to look at her.

She had decided not to be sad about not being able to have her father here to walk her down the aisle. Instead, she had tucked his letters in an envelope and wrapped them around the base of her bridal bouquet. She knew he was with her. She stepped forward and began walking down the aisle toward Geret.

Geret couldn't believe how beautiful his bride was. He couldn't believe that Lacey wanted to be with him, and he felt his eyes begin to water. *Thank you, Lord*, he thought. His eyes met Lacey's, and they were smiling at him. Joy filled his heart as he stepped forward to take her hand.

When the wedding ceremony was over, the reception was held outside under a white tent. The sun had set, and the tent was lit up with strings of twinkle lights. There was eating, drinking, laughing, music, and dancing. It made Lacey think of the wedding celebration when Jesus performed his first miracle and turned water to wine. Just like that day, she imagined that He was there with them. She knew He was. He had brought Geret into her life in His timing. He had required Lacey to trust Him, to take a leap of faith, and to move across the country. She was thankful that she had been obedient. She felt joy and contentment as she glanced around the tent at the people in her life. God had given her a family. She was finally home.

Denise Janette Bruneau

Denise Bruneau is a wife, mom, doctor, and writer. She resides in Kentucky with her husband, Mark, and her three children. She works as an OB Hospitalist, homeschools her youngest daughter, and writes in her spare time. She enjoys delivering babies, writing, reading, nature walks, exercise, and yoga.

Her first novel, Lavender Sky, was published in 2018. She loves to write love stories about life that are believable—stories that demonstrate God's love for people. She is a breast cancer survivor and loves the Lord with all of her heart.

1. What was your initial reaction to the book? Did it hook you immediately, or take some time to get into?

2. Do you think the story was plot-based or character driven?

3. What was your favorite quote/passage?

4. What made the setting unique or important? Could the story have taken place anywhere?

5. Did you pick out any themes throughout the book?

6. How credible/believable did you find the narrator to be? Did you feel like you got the 'true' story?

7. How did the characters change throughout the story? How did your opinion of them change?

8. Which character did you relate to the most, and what was it about them that you connected with?

9. How did you feel about the ending? What did you like, what did you not like, and what do you wish had been different?

10. Did the book change your opinion or perspective about anything? Do you feel different now than you did before you read it?

A Note from the Publisher

Dear Reader,

Thank you for reading Denise Janette Bruneau's novel, *Finding Home.*

We feel the best way to show appreciation for an author is by leaving a review. You may do so on any of the following sites:

www.ZimbellHousePublishing.com
Goodreads.com
or your favorite retailer

⊱⊰

Join our mailing list to receive updates on new releases, discounts, bonus content, and other great books from Denise Janette Bruneau and

Or visit us online to sign up
http://www.ZimbellHousePublishing.com